SECOND WIND
BOOK 3

THE CONNECTION

Suite 903, 600-22709
Lougheed Highway
Maple Ridge, V2X-0T5
www.TCJourney.com

Other Books in the
Spirit of the Game Series

SPIRIT OF THE GAME

SECOND WIND

BOOK 3

BY TODD HAFER

Zonder**kidz**

This book is dedicated to the life and memory of
Tim Hanson, a true athlete, a true friend.

Zonder**kidz**®

The children's group of Zondervan

www.zonderkidz.com

Second Wind
Copyright © 2004 by Todd Hafer

Requests for information should be addressed to:
Zonderkidz, Grand Rapids, Michigan 49530

Library of Congress Cataloging-in-Publication Data

Hafer, Todd.
  Second wind / by Todd Hafer.
    p. cm.–(The spirit of the game, sports fiction series)
  Summary: Fourteen-year-old Cody faces the challenge of track and field, a
school bully, and his father's new girlfriend.
  ISBN 0-310-70670-X (softcover)
  [1. Christian life—Fiction. 2. Friendship—Fiction. 3. Track and field—
Fiction.] I. Title.
  PZ7.H11975Se 2004
  [Fic]–dc22
                                             2004012664

Editor: Bruce Nuffer
Cover design Alan Close
Interior design: Susan Ambs
Art direction: Laura Maitner
Photos by Synergy Photographic
Printed in the United States of America

---

04 05 06 07 08/❖DC/5 4 3 2 1

Contents

Foreword

I love sports. I have always loved sports. I have competed in various sports at various levels, right through college. And today, even though my official competitive days are behind me, you can still find me on the golf course, working on my game, or on a basketball court, playing a game of pick-up.

Sports have also helped me learn some of life's important lessons–lessons about humility, risk, dedication, teamwork, friendship. Cody Martin, the central character in "The Spirit of the Game" series, learns these lessons too. Some of them, the hard way. I think you'll enjoy following Cody in his athletic endeavors.

Like most of us, he doesn't win every game or every race. He's not the best athlete in his school, not by a long shot. But he does taste victory, because, as you'll see, he comes to understand that life's greatest victories aren't reflected on a scoreboard. They are the times when you rely on a strength beyond your own —a spiritual strength—to carry you through. They are the times when you put the needs of someone else before your own. They are the times when sports become a way to celebrate the life God has given you.

So read on, and may you always possess the true Spirit of the Game.

Toby McKeehan

Chapter 1

Men Versus Mountain

"This is way worse than running suicides, Martin," Bart Evans groaned. "This is the kind of thing that could kill a guy for real! Dude, I thought he was tough as a hoops coach. But this is, like, another level of pain."

Eighth grader Cody Martin nodded grimly. *I'd rather run a hundred suicides than do this*, he thought. *Why did I let Coach Clayton talk me into this?* He rose up from his saddle as the road steepened. Each downstroke on the pedals of his 12-speed felt as if it would be his last. His quads burned, like they had been soaked in acid.

"If I peddle any slower," he mumbled, "I'll start going back downhill. I can't believe Coach made this sound fun."

Bart snorted weakly. "Coach Clayton is the devil. 'Scenic ride,' my foot, which is aching so bad I want to cut it off, by the way. 'Majestic ride, carving right through a historic Colorado mountain pass. Breathtaking rock walls so close to the road's edge you can reach out and touch them.'"

"Well," Cody offered, "it would be scenic, if we weren't blinded by pain."

The duo grew silent as they rounded a switchback and were hit by a stiff wind.

I should have suspected something when Coach Clayton dodged Gage's question, Cody thought. Gage McClintock, the track team's best 400-meter runner, had asked the distance coach, "Mountain pass, eh? I don't like the sound of that. How steep a mountain are we talkin' here?"

Coach Clayton, a six-foot-four scarecrow of a man, had laughed derisively. "Mac, don't be such a wimp. It's only a fourteen-mile ride. We're not talking about a leg of the Tour de stinkin' France. Not even a toe of the Tour de France. For cryin' out loud, I'm doin' the ride on my old mountain bike. You guys all have road bikes, so quit your whinin'."

"Besides," he added with a wink, "when we finish up in Woodland Park, I'm gonna buy you the best donuts anywhere. And then we get to ride *down*. I'm tellin' ya—you'll feel like you're flyin'!"

Flyin'? Cody thought. *A snail could crawl faster than this. I'm gonna topple over any second now, I just know it. It's just a matter of physics. It's not possible for a bike to go this slow.*

Cody knew that if he crashed, he was going to leave significant portions of his hide on Ute Pass. His cycling shoes were locked firmly in the toe clips, and he wouldn't have the time or energy to release them, especially if he biffed when he was up off the saddle. He raised his head to study the terrain ahead. His heart deflated like a balloon. Just ahead was the meanest hill of the ride.

It has to be two hundred yards long, Cody thought. *And it's straight up, no switchbacks!*

He heard himself whimper. Bart had pulled ten yards ahead of him moments earlier, but now Cody saw him maneuver his bike off the shoulder and execute an ungainly dismount. As he stood on the roadside, his legs buckled, and he had to lean on his bike for support.

"Forget this," Bart spat, as Cody ground by him. "I'm walking my bike up that monster hill. I'll walk it all the way to Woodland Park if I have to. My quads are Jell-O, dude."

"And if I live through this," he called to Cody as the distance between them stretched, "I'm gonna be a sprinter. No more of this distance stuff for me. It's too doggoned hard!"

Bart Evans, a sprinter? Cody smiled. *I don't think so. If you had any speed, dawg, you wouldn't be here.*

As Cody hit the hill's halfway point, he heard Bart again, his voice faraway and hollow— "What are you trying to prove anyway, Martin? What are you trying to proooove?"

I hate you Bart, he laughed to himself, grimly. *I was just about to get off my bike and walk too, and you have to go and say something like that. Now I have to keep going. What am I trying to prove? I don't know, but I guess I'll figure that out when I get to the top. If I get to the top.*

He was two-thirds up the hill now. He shifted his weight to his left and drove the pedal down, hoping to generate enough momentum to bring his foot back to the top position again. As he completed a slow revolution, his front wheel wobbled. Panic rippled through his body.

The panic was followed by a welcome rush of adrenaline—or maybe it was sunstroke. In either case, he clenched his jaw and willed himself to pick up his cadence.

I don't know if I'll ever get to the top of this hill, he resolved, *but I'll eat asphalt before I get off and walk.*

Cody closed his eyes and uttered a two-word prayer, "Strength—please." Then he blinked a drop of sweat from his left eye and began straining against the hill. *Only fifty yards to go, but I am so worked.*

He slumped back to his saddle. *Can't stay up anymore—legs will cramp if I do. But down on the saddle, I can't generate—any—power.*

Just as he was ready to give up, Cody felt a strong hand in the middle of his back, pushing him ahead. For a moment, he didn't have to strain alone against gravity and fatigue. Some benevolent force was aiding him.

Okay, I'm pretty sure this is a miracle, he thought. He glanced skyward. *When I begged for help, I didn't expect you to send a miracle, Lord, just a little more muscle power. But I'm glad you did. Thanks.*

"You're almost there, dude," a voice told Cody, "and once you crest this hill, it's candy."

Cody looked to his left. Drew Phelps removed his hand from Cody's back and made a fist. "Come on, Code. You're tougher than this mountain. Bring the pain."

"Bring the pain," Cody managed to wheeze in agreement. "Thanks, Phelps. For a minute there, I thought you were God."

"Do you really think the Lord would call you 'dude,' dude?"

"Maybe."

"Verily, verily, I say unto thee, dude—" Drew said with a chuckle.

"Thou art crazy, dude," Cody said.

Drew smiled and increased his speed. "Code," he called over his right shoulder as his thin but muscular legs churned like pistons, "go hard and count to twenty and you'll bust this hill. See you at the top."

Cody leaned forward as he began to count. He eyed the top of the hill. "Twenty more seconds," he whispered to the hill, "and you're mine. Well, mine and Drew's."

"You weren't lying about these donuts, Coach," Gage said, finishing his third honey whole wheat oval and brushing the golden crumbs off his legs.

Coach Clayton acknowledged the compliment by raising his blueberry muffin and saluting.

Cody and the rest of the Grant Junior High distance men flanked their coach at the Donut Mill's Liar's Table, the only table big enough to accommodate six eighth-grade tracksters and their lanky leader.

Cody shoved half a bear claw in his mouth and chased it down with a slug from his quart carton of chocolate milk. He watched Drew rise slowly to his feet and head to the front porch, which paralleled Woodland Park's main drag. He followed Drew out the door and they stood together, leaning on the porch rail, watching pickup trucks, dirt-encrusted Audis and Saabs, and the occasional Winnebago cruise by.

"Not a bad ride," Drew said. "A little short, but a decent workout all in all."

Cody wagged his head in disbelief. "You probably think root canals are a little short, too. I thought this was a way-hard way to begin the season. I thought I was in better shape."

Drew nodded. "I think that's Coach's plan. Help us see how far we have to go."

"Well, I have a *long* way to go."

"That's okay. Just be patient."

Cody studied his friend's face. "I guess you know all about patience," he said. "What was it like—being sick for almost a year?"

"It was like, uh, being sick. For almost a whole year. It was hard. But it was good for me."

Cody frowned. "Good?"

"It taught me to be patient. To pray, and wait for an answer. And it made me thankful for every mile, every step I had ever run. And I vowed that if—*when*—I could run again, I would treasure every step. Every dusty, lonely mile. Every race."

Cody stood upright, grabbed the porch rail with his left hand, and grabbed his right ankle with the other. Warily, he pulled his leg up and back, to stretch his quadriceps. He winced at the deep-set pain. "I'm glad I don't have to race right now. My legs are shot."

Drew turned toward Cody. "What doesn't kill you—"

"I know—makes me stronger. Believe me, I've said that a thousand times this past year."

"And you're still here."

"I guess so. Hey, thanks for the help back there. I really needed it. I wasn't sure I was going to make it."

Drew nodded slowly.

Cody laughed. "You could tell, huh? It was that obvious?"

Drew didn't answer, which was all the answer Cody needed. "I guess it's like Coach said during basketball, 'Fatigue makes cowards of us all.'"

Drew frowned and headed down the porch steps. He stretched his hands to the sky. The way he moved reminded Cody of a cat—relaxed—smooth.

They looked east, studying the pass they had just conquered. "I don't know that I agree with Coach," Drew said flatly. "Fatigue doesn't necessarily make you a coward. Fatigue can bring out the warrior in a person, if you know how to face it. If you're prepared for it."

"Well, I sure wasn't prepared. And I sure didn't feel like a warrior. I felt like a little old arthritic grampa, trying to climb Pikes Peak on a tricycle."

Drew took a long draw from his bottle of Gatorade. "But inside you, you had the warrior fire. You just needed a little spark to ignite it—or maybe reignite it. That's all I was trying to do. Start the spark. That's what my dad did for me, you know. When I finally got better, he went outside with me one day—May 6, to be exact. We ran, well, trotted to the end of the block. That was all. Then we walked back. But that was the start. That was the spark. That's what I was trying to do for you."

Cody shrugged and headed back up the stairs. "Well," he said, without looking over his shoulder at Drew, "it worked."

"Okay," Coach Clayton said, snapping the chinstrap of his helmet, "now comes the fun part—going down the mountain. But it won't be fun if I have to scrape anybody's carcass off Ute Pass. So, inexperienced riders, stay back. This isn't a race. Watch for patches of sand and gravel, and lay off the front brakes! Watch for the school van in a lot just before Manitou Springs."

Cody said a silent prayer for everyone's safety and climbed on his bike. He tucked behind Drew as the group began its descent.

As he whipped down the mountain, Cody began to feel small and vulnerable. The speed accentuated the road's many ruts and divots, and he had to clench his jaw to keep his upper and lower teeth from rattling against each other. He knew that one misread turn or one unfortunately placed rock would catapult him from his saddle. That was the danger. But that was also the thrill.

When the road finally leveled a bit, Cody called ahead to Drew, who was about three bike lengths ahead. "D," he said, drinking in the mountain air, "how fast?"

Drew looked at his handlebar-mounted computer and then shot a quick glance over his right shoulder. "We hit forty-two on that last steep grade. We're at thirty-one now. We passed that RV like it was standing still—did you see that?"

Before Cody could answer, Drew cut in. "Uh-oh, here come a bunch of S curves. Prepare thyself."

"I art prepared," Cody yelled, giving his rear brake lever two quick grabs to get his speed under control. Following Drew's lead, he shifted his weight, first to the left, and then to the right, staying low in the saddle, his eyes studying the jiggling terrain before him. He marveled at how deftly Drew controlled his coal-black Miyata 12-speed. He tried to mimic every lean and follow every angle.

Cody sighed when he saw the van parked in a crescent-shaped unpaved lot outside of Manitou. The downhill ride had ended too quickly. Coach Clayton was already securing his bike on top of the van. Gage was gulping hungrily from a bottle of Gatorade.

Cody and Drew whipped into the lot, side by side. Cody's bike began to fishtail when it hit the loose gravel, but he brought it under control and just missed making Gage a handlebar ornament.

Drew and Cody had already loaded their bikes and changed from their cycling shoes when Paul Getman and Mark Goddard arrived. "That was tight!" Goddard said.

Getman rolled his eyes. "So tight that you screamed like a girl going down Motel X hill?"

"I was screaming because I was into it. And it wasn't really a scream. It was a primal war cry."

Getman spat on the ground. "Well, you got the 'cry' part right, anyway. Your pants dry, Markie? You doughboy!"

Goddard pulled his bike even with Getman's, until the two of them were nose to nose. "You wanna check?"

"All right guys," Coach Clayton said, stepping between them. "I thought when basketball season was over, I wouldn't have to hear any more trash talking. You two better save your air for the season. Distance men need all the O-two they can get."

Then Coach paused and looked around the lot, rotating his head like a tank turret. "Hey, where's Evans?"

Goddard shrugged. "I thought he was up with you guys."

Cody saw the worry creep into his coach's wind-lashed face. "No," he said grimly, "I told him to stay at the back of the pack, but within contact." He drummed his fingers across his helmet, which he held in his left hand. "Okay, here's what we'll do. Martin, Phelps, you hop in the van with me. McClintock, you stay here with Goddard and Getman."

"Keep your eyes open, fellas," Coach Clayton said as he nursed the van through a series of switchbacks. "Drew, you and I will watch the eastbound lanes. Martin, you scour the westbound—in case Evans crossed over for some reason."

As the van crawled its way up the pass, Cody prayed earnestly, *Please, God, let Bart be okay. Please!*

As they passed by the small town of Cascade, Drew shouted, "Hey, Coach, I think I see him up ahead! See that skinny guy? Isn't that him sitting on the side of the road up there?"

Coach Clayton leaned over the steering wheel and studied the road ahead. "Yeah, that's Bart. He looks a little forlorn. Man, I hope he's okay."

"Well," Cody said hopefully, "at least he's sitting up and not lying flat out and unconscious."

Coach pulled the van off the right side of the road. Cody and Drew leaped out, and Cody looked down the pass. "Okay, we're clear. Let's go for it!"

The duo sprinted to a grassy median separating the east- and westbound lanes, waited for a Jeep to pass, and then hurried to Bart, who sat cross-legged against a reflector pole, his chin tucked against his chest. He was mouthing something—mostly unintelligible—although Cody could pick out the words, "Never, never again!"

Drew knelt in front of Bart. "Evans," he said softly, "are you all right? Are you hurt?"

Bart looked up. Cody could tell he had been crying. He had seen that kind of face in the mirror a thousand times during the past year—bloodshot eyes, hot, tear-streaked cheeks, runny nose.

"I'm okay, guys," Bart began slowly. "I'm just scraped up a little. I'm sorry if I worried anybody. Is Coach trippin' out about this?"

"Nah," Drew said. "He's just worried about you."

"Hey," Cody interjected, "where's your bike?"

Bart dipped his head backwards. "Down there. Somewhere."

Drew's eyes widened. "You rode down that steep embankment on your bike?!"

"No. I threw my bike down there—that's all."

Drew cocked his head. "Why?"

"Because I hate it, that's why. And I hate this whole trip!"

Cody and Drew helped Bart to his feet as the van approached, crunching its way over the loose gravel on the shoulder of the road.

"Sorry it took me so long, fellas," Coach Clayton said, bounding from the van. "Couldn't find a good place to turn around. What happened to you, Evans? Are you hurt? Should you be standing?"

"He's okay, Coach," Drew offered. "He just, uh—"

"I got a flat," Bart mumbled. "Then I kinda wrecked."

Coach Clayton's eyes widened. "And?"

"And I'm not hurt, not really." He held up the shredded palms of his bicycle gloves. "My gloves got the worst of it. Just don't ask me about my bike."

Coach looked puzzled. Cody mouthed the words, "He threw it," and Coach Clayton nodded, with a frown.

"I'll go get your bike," Drew offered. "Just tell me exactly where you tossed it."

"It's a bike, Phelps," Bart said, "not a Frisbee. How far do you think I could throw it?"

"Depends on how mad you were," Drew said, smiling.

Cody looked at Bart and knew he was trying to suppress a smile of his own.

Coach Clayton patted Bart lightly on the back. "We better clean and disinfect those scrapes on your arm and leg. They don't look bad, but we don't want them to get infected."

"Okay," Bart sighed. "And, hey, would it be too much to ask that you guys don't go blabbing this all over school next week?"

Cody and Drew looked at each other. "Yeah," Cody answered for both of them, "it would be too much to ask."

"Ha, ha, ha." Bart said, as he walked stiffly toward the van. Drew and Cody scrambled down the embankment to rescue Bart's bike, which had come to rest upside down, its wheels jutting toward the sky.

Chapter 2

Attacked!

Where's Coach taking us?" Cody asked Drew, his voice vibrating as Coach Clayton's dirty white Ford pickup rattled down County Road 8, heading west out of the small eastern-plains town of Grant, Colorado.

"It's not a question of where, it's a question of how far. I mean, he dropped Goddard off five minutes ago. And it's been two minutes since the rest of 'em got out. It will be hard to catch them."

"Hard? Try impossible."

Drew shot Cody such a fierce look that he turned away from its heat. "We'll catch them," Drew said evenly. "There's no question."

Cody didn't doubt Drew Phelps when it came to running. He had learned that last year.

Drew had moved to Grant at the beginning of seventh grade. Cody was assigned to be his "buddy," showing him around the school and "introducing him to some of the fellas," as Principal Prentiss put it, in his steadfastly uncool way.

Cody had studied Drew as they stood in the principal's office on the first day of school. *He's even skinnier than I am*, Cody thought. But the new kid looked like a jock of some sort. Tall. Hard, ropy muscles. Deep tan. And there was something about the way he carried himself. Relaxed. Loose-limbed. Kind of like Terry Alston, the best all-around athlete in the school.

"Okay, all-righty then," Mr. Prentiss was saying. "You're all set, Mr. Phelps. Cody Martin here will show you around this week and help you get settled in. Cody, this is Drew Phelps, a new student from Wyoming."

Drew's handshake was unsettlingly firm.

Cody made himself tall. "Nice to meet you, Drew."

"Same here."

"So, you're from Wyoming. What part?"

"Buffalo. It's a small town in the northeast part."

"Smaller than Grant?"

"Yeah, I'm pretty sure. We only have about four thousand people in the whole town."

"Huh. You do sports up there?"

"Track and a little bit of basketball."

Cody thought for a moment. "You any good?"

"Basketball—I have a ways to go. In track, I'm all right. I'm a distance man."

"Yeah? Cool. You'll have to meet Gage McClintock. Last year, as a sixth grader, he was the second-fastest guy on the varsity team—you know, the eighth graders! He ran the mile in under six minutes. Five-fifty-something. It's a record for sixth graders. Broke the old one by, like, twenty seconds."

Drew smiled slightly. "Oh."

Cody didn't understand the smile until a week later. Coach Smith, the head football coach who also taught PE, took his fourth-period class to the track to run a timed mile. "We need to assess your physical condition," he explained to his students. "You don't have to try to keep up with Mr. McClintock here, but I want you to do your best."

"That's Gage," Cody whispered to Drew. "The guy with the red hair. He's the one I was telling you about. He won a few varsity races last year. If you can keep up with him, you'll be doing great. But don't put too much pressure on yourself. He's a stud."

Drew smiled again.

Cody left him there to search out Pork Chop and Mark Goddard. "Hey, dudes," he said, "you wanna run together? I'm sure not going to run with Gage. He's a mutant."

Deke "Pork Chop" Porter was stretching his thick left leg on a hurdle. "I know. But you better not run with me. I'll slow you down. I'm not built for this kinda thing. Besides, you know those little powdered-sugar donuts?"

"Uh, yeah."

"Well, I ate a whole box of them for breakfast."

"Chop, I thought you were going to try to cut down on that kinda junk."

Pork Chop smiled sheepishly. "Yeah, I know. But those little things are so tasty. Hey, by the way, what's the new guy's name again?"

"Drew Phelps," Cody said. "He's from Wyoming. Says he plays hoop. Runs track, too. Distance."

"Really?" Goddard said, arching his thin, blond eyebrows. "Is he any good?"

"I don't know. He might be pretty good. He seems to be built for distance."

"Come on, Code! We can take him. How good can he be? He's from Wyoming."

"I don't know, Mark, there's something about him."

"Look, let's stay behind him for the first three laps and then smoke him."

"Okay. Sounds like a plan to me."

"Sounds stupid to me," Pork Chop said with a belch. "I'll leave you guys to it. Me and my stomach full of donuts are going to find a nice, comfortable place at the back of the pack."

Coach Smith lined up thirty boys at the starting line. "Let's have a good run, fellas." He patted Gage on the head. "Anybody beats the smooth-running red-head here, I buy him a pizza."

Most of the students laughed. Cody, standing to Gage's immediate left, felt a hand on his shoulder.

"Excuse me," Drew said. "But I need to get in front of the pack."

Cody studied the new guy's blue-green eyes.

"I don't want to run anybody over."

Cody shook his head and extended his arm, like an usher at church. "Be my guest."

"Hey, Gage," someone called from the pack. "The new guy's gonna challenge you!"

Gage turned to see Drew taking a place beside him. Gage smirked and spat on the infield grass.

On Coach Smith's command, Drew shot from the line, at what seemed to be a full sprint. Gage settled in behind him. After one lap, they had fifty yards on the pack. "What was that about smoking the new guy?" Cody gasped at Goddard.

"Change in plans. But I bet Gage buries him. Look, he's staying right on his heels."

"Yeah, but he's straining, look. That dude, Drew almost looks like he's enjoying himself."

"They're both mutants. Can't—can't talk anymore."

Cody watched Gage chase Drew through lap two and then lap three. As the duo passed Coach Smith, who was staring at his stopwatch in disbelief, Gage moved to Drew's right shoulder. Drew glanced at him briefly and broke into a full sprint. In comparison, Gage appeared to be wading through gelatin.

Drew catapulted out of the first turn and had twenty yards on Gage by the time he entered the final turn.

Gage tired so badly that Cody nearly caught him in the last 100 meters. But Gage must have felt him coming on, because he summoned one last burst of speed to hold off Cody and then collapsed across the finish line.

"Five-forty-four, Mac," Coach Smith said evenly. "Not bad for the off-season. And hey, Cody—only three seconds behind Gage. Coach Haynes is gonna want you out for track."

Coach Smith was interrupted by Drew, who appeared only slightly winded, as if he'd just climbed a few flights of stairs. "Excuse me, sir. Can you tell me what my time was?"

"Yeah! I wanted to earlier, but you sprinted across the line and just kept running!"

"My warm-down," Drew said quietly.

"Son, you aren't warm—you're hot! You just ran a 5.30 mile. That's faster than the seventh grade school record! Of course, this wasn't a track meet, so you don't get the record."

Drew nodded. "But I do get a pizza."

Coach Smith laughed. "Any kind you want."

Drew jogged to the high jump pit as Coach Smith urged the straggling milers to hurry up. Cody waited for Goddard to trudge across the line, and then the two of them joined Drew at the pit. Cody let himself fall backwards onto the thick, blue mat, next to Drew.

"Nice run, man," Cody said. "I don't think Gage has ever lost to a Grant runner."

"Thanks. But I'm not in very good shape yet. Haven't done much speed work."

"Mutant," Goddard whispered.

Drew sat up slowly. "Hey, since the coach owes me a pizza, how would you guys like to join me after school, Cody and, uh, Mark, right?"

Cody looked at Goddard. "Yeah, he's Mark, and as you can see from the little spare tire, he loves pizza. But, you know, you can't get a decent pizza in this town. You have to go to the Springs for that. But if you want a good burger, you can go to Big Al's, Dairy Delight, or Mamie's House o' Pies."

"Louie's makes a good pizza," Goddard offered.

Cody thought for a moment. "Yeah, I guess so."

Just then, Pork Chop entered the turn near the high jump area. "Never again," he said, coughing and sputtering like an old tractor. "Those little donuts are evil."

Cody smiled. "You're almost done, Chop. Sprint it in."

"Ha, ha, ha. Sprinting is against my religion."

"Not when it's dinnertime."

"If I don't die," Pork Chop called back over his shoulder, "I'm comin' back to pummel you, Martin."

The three distance men studied Pork Chop as he lumbered toward the finish.

"Actually," Drew noted, "he runs pretty well for a big dude. His form isn't bad."

"He's a monster in football—basketball, too. He not only looks like Charles Barkley, he plays like him," Goddard said. "And he says he's going to throw the shot and disc in track this year. I bet he heaves the shot a mile."

"Come on," Cody said, rolling off the mat, "let's head over to the finish line, in case Chop needs CPR."

"If he does," Goddard said, "he's all yours."

Pork Chop was standing on the track, fingers laced behind his head, as Drew offered his hand.

"Nice to meet you, Drew," Pork Chop said. "Great run, I think. That was you who won, wasn't it? My vision got kinda blurry on account of the acute exhaustion and excruciating pain I was in."

"Yeah," Drew said, trying to stifle a smile. "That was me."

"I bet Gage is mad. He always wins whenever that sadist Smith makes us run the mile."

"He'll get used to it."

Pork Chop burst into laughter, which turned into another coughing fit. "Whoa, Code, check this guy out. He's got some serious bravado!"

"I'm just stating the fact," Drew said. "By the way, since I won a pizza, I'd like to invite the three of you to join me for dinner tonight. What's the name of that place, Mark?"

"It's Louie's, but if Pork Chop is coming with us, you better ask Coach Smith to spring for two pizzas."

Pork Chop scratched his head. "But then what will you guys eat?"

"Chop," Cody said, "I thought you were hurtin' because of those little donuts."

"Well, pizza has always soothed my stomach. It has, you know, medicinal qualities or something. Especially when it's free." He nodded toward Drew. "Thanks for the invite, dawg. You can count me in."

And so the legend of Drew Phelps was born. He officially shattered the seventh-grade record for the mile, which was five minutes, thirty-nine seconds, at the first meet of the season. He ran a 5.28, which also bettered the eighth-grade school record of 5.29. But after finishing more than 20 seconds ahead of his nearest competitor, he took off his Nike spikes and threw them against the chain-link fence surrounding the track. He wanted the eighth-grade conference record, too, which he missed by fifteen seconds. "Stupid cold," he said. "I couldn't breathe. That was a terrible race."

"But you broke two school records," noted Cody, who finished third. "And you're only in seventh grade."

Drew glared at him. "I wanted three records."

Gage, meanwhile, knew the Distance King crown had been wrested from him. He abandoned the longer distances in favor of the 400 meters.

Cody looked across the pickup bed at Drew, who now had the three records he craved, and then some. Last year, as a seventh grader, Drew bettered the junior high conference mark in the third meet of the season, officially lowering it to 5.02 at conference championships, where he lapped half the field. Once again, he flung his shoes—this time off the side of the Grant bus, because he failed to break the five-minute barrier.

Two weeks into the eighth grade season, however, Drew seemed calmer. Just as focused, but not as angry as before.

"I think Coach is slowing down," Drew noted as the truck angled toward the shoulder.

"With the way his truck vibrates, you sound like a billy goat," Cody said.

"Yeah? Well, you sound like a quivery-voiced old grandma."

Cody was forming his verbal counterpunch when Coach Clayton must have leg-pressed his brake pedal to the floorboard. The sudden stop threw Cody across the pickup bed like a football.

Drew, with a kung fu grip on the side rail, managed to spare himself the same fate.

"Martin," Coach Clayton snapped, leaning his head out the window. "Out!"

"Just a sec, Coach. I'm checking for broken bones. Who taught you how to drive, anyway?"

"You want to ride another mile with Phelps, Martin?"

"No sir."

"Then jump out and start stridin'."

Cody grasped the tailgate with both hands and whipped his legs over the truck's back end. He landed lightly on the shoulder, looking to Drew for approval on the perfect dismount. But his smile quickly vanished when Coach Clayton gunned his engine, popped the clutch, and peppered him with dirt and gravel.

Cody could hear Drew's and Coach's laughter fading away as he turned and began a slow jog back toward town, spitting dirt and dabbing his eyes with the inside of his shirt as he went.

As he ran, Cody began calculating his chances of not finishing dead last in this "crucial" (in Coach Clayton's words) training run. He figured they had dispatched Goddard about three miles from town— then Getman, Gage, and Bart at about four miles. He looked at his watch. He was between a quarter and a third of a mile behind the McClintock trio.

Goddard was tenacious but exhibited all the speed of a glacier. It would take him more than thirty minutes to reach the school. The rest of the guys would take thirty-six minutes to finish. Cody figured Gage might push them to a little faster time, but he was still recovering from a sore hamstring, and Cody knew he wouldn't do anything to risk further injury. In fact, he was surprised that the ultra-cautious runner was practicing at all.

Cody processed the numbers in his head. He'd have to average a 7.5-minute mile to finish in just under thirty-two minutes.

Uh-oh, he thought, *that means there's no way to catch Goddard. The pack, though, they're catchable. They have more than a half-mile lead right now, counting the time in the truck. They're probably about three and a-quarter miles from school right now. I must be about four even. So, if I can run a 7.15 pace, I'll get 'em. At least I think so. Man, math is hard—especially when you're running!*

Cody picked up his pace, his eyes and throat now clear of the dirt. He sensed someone behind him. He rotated his head and saw Drew, about forty yards back and gobbling the distance between them with his quick, smooth strides.

Man! he thought. *Here comes the mutant.*

"Hey, Code," Drew's voice was strong, "wait up, will ya?"

Drew arrived on Cody's right shoulder within moments. "Very funny, Phelps. You're just killing me with that sense of humor. How much farther did Coach drive you, anyway?"

"Just another quarter mile or so."

"Hmm," Cody said, trying to disguise the fact that he was already gulping for air. "What took you so long then?"

"Shoe came untied. Had to stop."

"Please tell me you're kidding."

"Okay, I'm kidding."

Cody felt a painful knot forming in his right side. "Drew, I don't know if I'm built for this distance stuff."

"Sure you are. You're a natural runner. I've told you that."

"That's not what I feel like right now."

Cody felt Drew studying him.

"You're too tight."

"Huh?"

"Your hands are clenched. Your jaw is set. Relax, shake your arms out. Let your jaw drop, like you just saw Robyn Hart in her homecoming dress."

"Give me a break."

"Okay. I'm just trying to loosen you up, dude. Don't strain, Code. Just stride. Float. Let your feet barely kiss the ground."

"Kiss the ground? Are you for real?"

"I'm as real as it gets. Look, running can be like flying. Like floating. But you gotta find your rhythm. You gotta glide over the ground. Not pound on top of it."

"Glide?"

"Yeah. Look, just keep up with me, okay? But don't think about it. Don't strain. Just do as I do. Just enjoy the flight."

Cody saw Drew rise on his toes and pick up the pace. He fought the compulsion to grit his teeth, and churn his arms and legs. Instead, he focused on mirroring Drew's smooth, seemingly effortless strides.

It felt good.

Drew looked at Cody and smiled encouragingly. Then he found another gear and accelerated.

Cody lengthened his stride and again fell into rhythm with the area's best long-distance runner— for about thirty seconds.

As the duo headed up a gradual incline, Cody felt his legs growing heavy. His footfalls changed from soft, quick scuffs to heavy *slap, slaps*. He shook his head and slowed to a jog.

"Glide," he gasped. "Yeah, right."

With a ballet dancer's ease, Drew turned around and began running backwards, easily keeping up with Cody. "Don't get discouraged, Code. You were going great. As you get stronger, you'll be able to hold that form longer."

"You mean, like, for a whole minute or something?"

"A minute's not a bad short-term goal. Then two. Then you'll be doing a whole mile like that. And that will be cool, because—"

"Because what?"

"Because of a secret I'm about to tell you."

"What? You're really nineteen?"

"No. You know how fast we were going back there?"

"How fast?"

"Sub-five pace, homeboy."

Cody let the news bounce around in his head, like a racquetball. "For real? Sub-five?"

"I wouldn't lie about a milestone like that."

"Unbelievable. I didn't think I could do that, even for a little while."

"Now you know you can. How did it feel?"

"It rocked! You know, that's faster than the district record. It's 5.01."

Drew grinned confidently. "For the moment it is."

After telling Cody, "Don't keep plodding along—run! Work hard—this is where you get strong!" Drew dashed away in pursuit of the remainder of the Grant distance team.

Cody arrived at the school last, but only about twenty-five yards behind Gage and his pack. Outside the rear entrance to the gym, he saw Coach Clayton, slapping Drew on the back as if trying to dislodge a steak bone from his gullet.

"Now that's what I call running, Mr. Phelps. For the love of Jim Ryun, you were just flyin'! I can't believe you ran down Goddard and the whole lot of 'em. Whipped by 'em like they were traffic cones!"

Drew chugged the remainder of a bottle of Gatorade. "Thanks, Coach. But Goddard did fight to hold me off. He's got guts."

Coach Clayton grinned. "And deceptive speed, too."

Drew shot the coach a puzzled look. "Deceptive speed?"

"Yeah. He's a lot slower than he looks."

Drew laughed politely and then noticed Cody approaching.

"Good run, Code," he said. "You're gonna be tough before the season's over. Hey, Coach—Cody and I put in some sub-five work out there. He hung right with me."

"Maybe for a while," Coach Clayton said, glancing at his watch, "but then what happened, Martin? You lose your way? Or stop to pick daisies for a certain girl sprinter?"

Cody smiled nervously. "Aww, Coach, c'mon. Give me a break. I really did try. It's just that trying to keep up with Flash Phelps here took too much outta me. But I'm not making excuses. I'm last, and I know I have to go push your truck once around the track now, like you threatened before practice."

Coach Clayton interlaced his twiggy fingers and cracked his knuckles. "Nah, you don't have to push Betty around the track. I make exceptions to my rules for anyone who can run sub-five pace, even for a minute or two. So, go shower, Martin. I can smell the stank comin' off of you from here."

After politely refusing Drew's offer to stop at Dairy Delight for a post-practice milk shake, Cody waited for Coach Clayton to go into the gym and then jogged the quarter mile from the school to the track, which was located directly behind Grant High School, next-door neighbor to the middle school.

He grinned when he saw Pork Chop in the shot put ring, working on his release.

"Hey, Code," Chop grunted as he released the metal ball high into the air. "You wanna be my shot put catcher for a while?"

"I only catch javelins, you know that, Chop."

"How was your run?"

"Loooong. Too long." Cody turned from Pork Chop and studied the track, which was due west of the throwing area.

"She's not up there, dawg. They finished twenty minutes ago."

"I wasn't looking for Robyn, dude. I was just—lookin'. You know?"

"Oh, I know, all right."

"You think you know. Look, how much longer are you gonna throw?"

"Give me ten more minutes, max. I need to really launch one. I haven't had a monster throw all afternoon. I'm all outta sync. I think Doug messed up my arm when we were wrestling around last night. "Big brothers—who needs 'em?"

Cody felt his stomach rumble. "Well, I'm gonna bounce then, I guess. I'm hungry. I was gonna see if you wanted to have a burger with me, but I can't wait."

"Burger, huh? Okay, then. Give me just a couple more throws. Why don't you go run a lap or something to cool down?"

"I'm not running another step. I'm cooked. We ran, like, four-plus miles today. Some at sub-five pace."

"You're frontin'! Sub-five-minute-mile pace? I couldn't run that fast, even if a bear was chasin' me!"

"I'm not frontin', Chop. Ask Phelps. He paced me."

"You kept up with that psycho? I'm impressed."

With that, Pork Chop bent his knees, nestled the shot put under the right side of his jaw then exploded with a fierce "Arrrrgh!" Cody marveled at the heavy ball's trajectory. It reminded him of a free throw—a smooth, high-arcing parabola.

The ball landed with a dull whump in the wet sand, about fifteen paces from the shot put ring.

"Yeah!" Pork Chop exulted. "Now that's what I'm talkin' about. That's out there beyond forty feet!"

He turned to Cody and belched deeply. "Now we can eat!"

Cody and Pork Chop had walked about half the distance from Grant Middle School to Dairy Delight when it approached them—a blue Ford pickup barreling their way, churning up a cloud of dust behind it.

Just another high school idiot trying to prove his manhood, Cody thought. But then he saw the bottles hurtling toward them. One shattered at Pork Chop's feet, causing both of them to jump backward. The first bottle had come from the driver's side. The second, from the passenger side, followed it by only a second or two. This one whipped past Cody's eyes, so close that he noted the Budweiser label.

Instinctively Cody crouched, trying to pull Pork Chop down with him.

As the truck roared away, Cody rose warily. "What was up with that?"

Pork Chop's voice was shaky. "I . . . I . . . don't know. Did you get a license number or anything?"

"Are you kiddin'? I was too busy ducking."

"Me, too. Code, my heart's doing a drum solo. That was trippy!"

"Yeah. You can say that again. I don't think I've seen that truck before. You?"

"No, why?"

"Well, after hoops season ended, that thug Gabe Weitz kinda tried to run me down when I was running home one night. But he was driving a beat-up old

Nova. Remember that guy your brother KO'd with one punch?"

Pork Chop kicked at the ground. "Of course, I remember. Hmm. I wonder if Weitz traded his car in. Or maybe he was in a friend's ride this time. In any case, I gotta tell Doug about this. And if it was Weitz, there won't be any one-punch KO this time. He's gonna regret he harassed us again. Because this time, he is gonna suffer! I can hardly wait to see it."

Cody shook his head slowly. "Chop, you can't tell Doug."

"Why?"

"Because he *will* tear Weitz apart. And then he'll get kicked out of school, and then he'll lose his scholarship. Hasn't he used up all his warnings this year?"

"Yeah," Pork Chop muttered. "He shoulda paced himself better. Too many fights too early in the year. Too many pranks. You're right, Code. I can't tell him. There's no way he could hold himself back from sending Weitz to the ER."

"So, I guess it's up to us, if it is Weitz who's stalking us."

"You got any ideas?"

Cody shrugged.

"Looks like I have to be the brains of this outfit once again," Pork Chop said. "Lucky for you I haven't used up all my mental power in school."

"So, what's your plan, oh mastermind?"

"Well, first we eat."

"You're still hungry—after nearly getting nailed like that?"

Pork Chop rubbed his stomach affectionately, as if it were a pet. "Are you kiddin'?"

After Cody and Pork Chop finished dinner, Chop phoned his brother and begged for a ride home. On the ride home when Doug asked the duo in the car how track practice went, they looked at each other for a moment before Pork Chop said, "Boring."

Cody entered his house to find his dad, his hair mussed, sitting in his recliner and reading the *Wall Street Journal*. CNN was on the TV, but the sound was muted. Cody headed for the kitchen, but stopped when his dad announced from behind his paper, "You're late. Very late."

"Sorry, Dad," Cody muttered before resuming his trek to the refrigerator.

"Sit down," his father snapped, folding the paper and dropping it on the floor.

Cody obeyed, sitting on the floor in front of the recliner.

"Cody, it's now 7:15. I told you this morning that we were going to have dinner together tonight. I told you to be home by 6:30."

Cody swallowed nervously. "I'm sorry, Dad. I totally spaced it. It's just that you usually work late, and I end up sitting here every night chowing down on some microwave meal. So when Chop asked me to have a burger with him—"

Cody saw his dad's pale-blue eyes narrow. "I work hard to support you. I work overtime. I know that my job requires a lot of me, but welcome to the real world, son. Besides, you're confusing the issue here. We are not going to discuss my work hours—again. We're going to discuss your failure to be where I told you to be tonight."

"I already apologized, Dad. I just plain forgot. It's not like I deliberately disobeyed you."

"So you say."

"What's that supposed to mean? Are you calling me a liar, Dad? You know I'm not like that, don't you? I promise I'm telling the truth. Go get your Bible and put me under oath." Cody dipped his head, studying a grape-juice stain on the carpet. "Or do you even know where your Bible is anymore?"

Cody noticed his dad's foot begin to tap rapidly, as it always did when he was anxious—or angry.

Cody's father seemed to be trying to keep his voice from quaking. "You better not forget, son, who is in charge here," he said, running his hand through his thick ash-colored hair. "That kind of comment is out of line. Besides, my spiritual life is my business, not yours. The sooner you accept that fact, the better both of our lives will be."

Cody exhaled sadly. "I'm sorry, Dad. I really am. I just worry that you just seem to have cut God out of your life."

"Well, he cut my wife out of my life, so I guess we're even."

"But, Dad, the cancer wasn't God's doing," Cody said. "Please don't be mad at him."

"Well, to tell the truth, I'm more mad at you right now."

"I know, and I guess I deserve it. I'll remember better next time. And I'm sorry for bustin' your chops about your Bible."

Cody watched his dad, struggling with his anger, as he probably counted to ten in his head. That's what Mom had always told him to do. Finally, his dad's shoulders relaxed and he sighed.

"Okay. But you could have called me, Cody. I would understand if you preferred to eat with Pork Chop. I know I'm not very good company right now."

"Well, I'm not exactly Mr. Congeniality, either."

Cody's father stood and stretched his arms toward the ceiling, uttering that gorilla-esque grunt dads are so good at. "Let's just learn from tonight and move on. You can change the TV channel if you want. I'm going to put the leftovers away."

"Leftovers? Dad, you cooked?"

Cody's father forced a smile. "No, I ordered Chinese."

Cody passed on the kung pao chicken offered to him, but he did eat both fortune cookies, without looking at either fortune. His mom had always said, "Only God knows the future, and if he wanted us to know, he would have adopted the fortune cookie concept himself, not let Confucius have it."

Right before he headed upstairs, Cody replayed the beer-bottle incident in his head. He stared at his dad, who was back in front of the TV.

"Hey, Dad?" he said.

"Yes? Is something wrong?"

"Uh—no. I guess not."

"You sure? If you're having a problem at school or something, I'm here to help."

Cody noticed that his dad's eyes hadn't left the TV set during the entire conversation.

"Nah, everything's fine," he said.

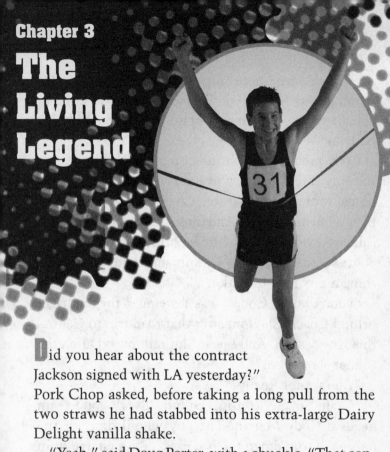

Chapter 3
The Living Legend

"Did you hear about the contract Jackson signed with LA yesterday?" Pork Chop asked, before taking a long pull from the two straws he had stabbed into his extra-large Dairy Delight vanilla shake.

"Yeah," said Doug Porter, with a chuckle. "That contract had more zeros than one of our family reunions, Chop."

"I'll never make that kinda paper," Cody said ruefully.

Pork Chop, who sat across the booth from Cody, belched in protest. "You can't think that way, dawg. We are gonna make the big time. We *will* go to the Show. I'm gonna be the best D-lineman the Broncos have ever had. And you, if you can put on some muscle, will be one tough cornerback, or maybe a strong safety. Or, who knows? Maybe you'll hit a growth spurt and be able to play hoops. You got options. You got skills. We both do!"

Cody nibbled thoughtfully on a French fry. "About the only career options I'm gonna be talking about will be 'paper or plastic.' Get real, Chop. I'm not fast enough to be a DB in the NFL. And those NBA teams, they just salivate over skinny white small forwards with six-point scoring averages. I think somebody put something funny in your shake."

"I don't know, Code. I was sleeping in the bus, right behind Coach Clayton, after that road trip to Central this past season. And I hear him talkin' to Dutch the trainer about you."

"About me? Really?"

"Yeah. So, he's telling Dutch, 'Every good team needs a Cody Martin. The guy who'll dive for the loose ball, run down the bad pass, take a charge from a guy twice his size. The guy who just doesn't make mistakes—and doesn't care about his stats. The guy who doesn't care about anything but giving his all for his team.'"

"Coach really said that? Come on!"

"Those are pretty much his exact words."

"Well, how come you never told me before this?"

Pork Chop slurped from his shake, sat back in the booth, and smiled contentedly. "Mainly because I wished Coach had been saying those things about *me*. I kept pretending to be asleep the whole trip, but do you think he threw one prop my way? Nada. So I guess I was kinda jealous of you. Besides, I didn't want you to get the big head."

"Yeah," Doug broke in. "One big head is quite enough between the two of you."

"Hey, there's a fine line between being cocky and being confident, big brutha."

"And you're standing about fifty feet on the wrong side of it," Doug said.

Pork Chop was formulating a comeback when he must have noticed Cody, wagging his head in disbelief.

"What's up, Code. You hear something good about yourself, and it rocks your whole world?"

"It just doesn't compute, Chop. I mean, I work hard and everything, but—"

"It should compute, Code," Doug said. "Look right here in our own state. The Nuggets have almost always had a guy like you—Dunn, Hanzlik, Bowen. They never got on the cover of *Sports Illustrated*, but they all had good, long careers. And the fans loved 'em. Because they were gritty. Because they played hard."

Cody finished his 7-UP. "But weren't those guys superstars in college?"

Doug looked Cody in the eye. "What do you think? They were blue-collar college players who kept working hard and became solid pros. Could be you someday."

"Whoa. I'd love to play pro ball, but it's really been nothing more than a stupid dream. I mean, do you know what those guys make? Even the league minimum is more than three times what my dad will ever pull in."

"Yeah," Pork Chop said, flicking a potato chip shard off the table, "but I'm not settling for minimum. I'm talkin' millions. Fat stacks o' green. I'm gonna have a private jet and at least three homes. One near here, so I can be close to the Old Boy. One up in Aspen, for ski season. And one on the beach in San Diego."

"I don't know which is scarier, little brother," Doug noted, "the thought of you on skis, or the sight of you in a Speedo, lyin' on the sand like a walrus."

"You're trippin', DP. I'm not gonna have this baby fat forever, you know. When I'm up in the Show, I'm gonna hire a personal trainer and be cut like one of those Greek statues."

"Well, if you want to be all sculpted, you're gonna have to lay off the milk shakes and such. So—" Doug snatched the cup from in front of his brother— "I'm doing this for the good of your career."

"Hey! Give me my shake."

Doug placed the cup on the far end of the table, turned toward Pork Chop, grabbed him by both shoulders, and shook vigorously. "There you go, little brother. There's your shake."

With an air of feigned indignation, Pork Chop straightened his shirt. "See if I give you any of my comp fifty-yard-line tickets," he sniffed. "You'll regret this when I'm All-World. I'll tell ESPN how you punked me out. Then they'll come down to McDonald's, so you can take off your paper hat and tell me and the world how sorry you are."

Doug stood and began gathering the table trash. "Keep dreamin', little brother. Keep dreamin'."

"Hey, DP," Cody said, "Chop has me thinking—what about *your* pro career? I mean, it seems like you could play football, be a DH in baseball, or even be one of those professional wrestlers."

"I don't know, Code."

"But everybody in town talks about it. They're sure you'll be the first guy in the history of the town to be a pro athlete."

"Yeah," Pork Chop chimed in, "you got it made. You're the king in this town! All-state four times in football? Even I might not make varsity till my sophomore year. And two state titles in wrestling—

Code, you should see all the packets this meathead gets from schools all over the country. And I'm talkin' Big 12, Big Ten, PAC–10, not Tumbleweed Junior College and stuff like that."

Cody studied Doug, who shook his head slowly, a small smile creasing his face. "College," Doug said wistfully.

"Of course," Pork Chop said, holding the exit door for his two dining companions, "Doug doesn't really even need college. He can just tear it up for a year or two and then jump to the NFL. He won't need a college degree. He'll major in *football*!"

"Actually," Doug said as he unlocked his Camry, "I'm going to major in secondary education. And I will graduate, Chop. And you and Cody better plan on doing the same."

"Get real, DP," Pork Chop countered as he lowered himself into the front passenger seat. "You know I hate school, and I'm gonna go only as long as I have to. I'm not gonna bust my tail for four or five years just so I can get some crummy job that pays, like, thirty grand a year. I'm not built for that. With my NFL signing bonus and salary, I'll make enough in one year to be set for life!"

Pork Chop turned to Cody, who sat in the middle of the backseat. "And, Co, don't worry if you don't make it to the Show. I got your back. You can be my agent or something. Just think, even eight percent of a $60-million contract would be—uh, a lot. It'd be a lot."

"It would be $4.8 million, dipstick," Doug said quietly. "And you're blowing a lot of smoke about money you don't have."

"Not yet. But it'll happen, my brutha."

Doug drummed his fingertips on his steering well. He glanced at Cody via the rearview mirror. "Little man, you in a hurry to get home?"

"No, not really."

"Good. Then we're gonna take a little field trip."

"Doug," his brother protested, "can't we just go home? I might be missing something cool on TV."

Doug sighed heavily and drove from the parking lot. After a few moments, he asked, "Cody, you ever hear of Grant Walken?"

"Rock Walken? Of course. I've seen all the articles and photos in the trophy case at the high school. And he practically owns the Wall of Fame. My mom used to say that the town was named after him, not the other way around."

"Yeah, he's a legend," Pork Chop said. "Whatever happened to him, anyway? Didn't he go play football up in Canada or something? Or was it basketball in Spain?"

"You're about to find out what happened to him," Doug answered quietly.

Cody watched the chewed-up wooden stairs bend and creak under Doug Porter's weight. *You shoulda gone up ahead of him*, Cody told himself. *At least that way, if the stairs collapse, you'd land on him, not the other way around.*

When they arrived at apartment "M", Doug pounded the door with the meaty part of his fist.

"Come in, unless you're selling something or I owe you money," Cody heard a muffled voice call.

Doug twisted the doorknob and led his two charges inside.

"The morning always gets here too soon," Rock Walken grumbled from the bathroom.

Pork Chop looked at Cody and rolled his eyes. "It's one o'clock in the afternoon," he whispered. Then he plucked a book, which lay face-down on an old brick-red ottoman. Turning it over, he saw it was a nine-year-old Grant High School yearbook. A page was marked with a long-expired Pizza Hut coupon. It was the introduction to the sports section.

Cody smiled at the full-page picture, opposite the words "Grant Sports." It was the same picture that adorned the Wall of Fame. Grant Walken at full speed. His blonde hair flying behind him. His face lean and smooth. The ball in total submission to his skilled right hand.

"Man, I love that picture." Walken was standing in front of them, dressed in old gray gym shorts. His chest was sunken, and his gelatinous belly hung lifelessly over his waistband. His once sinewy biceps were long gone. His hair was still long, but when he bent down to get a closer look at the picture, Cody noted a bald spot the size of a silver dollar hiding under a thin crosshatch of greasy yellow strands.

"Remember that game? It was against Saint Stephen's. I had thirty-eight."

"I remember," Doug assured him. "I was there, sitting right behind the bench. If Rice hadn't taken you out of the game early in the fourth, you mighta cracked fifty."

Walken scratched his chest. "Oh, baby! Half a hundred in a high school game! That woulda been sweet!" He moved to the refrigerator. "You guys want something to eat?"

"Nah," Doug answered. "That's okay."

"You sure? I've got some weenies—and something in a bag. No wait, I don't think this is good anymore. But hey, I have beer! Anybody feel like breaking training?"

"Rock," Doug said. "I never break training. And these guys don't even shave yet, much less drink beer. Look, dude, we just came from the double-D. We're not hungry. We're not thirsty. Save the beer and weenies—in case there's a famine."

"Okay. I'm just trying to be, you know, hostile and all."

Doug appeared ready to correct Walken, but then held his tongue.

The past, present, and future of Grant High athletics took turns exchanging glances.

After about a minute of awkward silence, Walken shrugged and tapped a quick drum solo on his ample belly. "Okay. I guess I'll get dressed. That'll give you guys time to figure out what in the world you're doing here." He turned toward his bedroom.

"He looks like Hulk Hogan, before the steroids," Pork Chop whispered.

Doug glared at his brother and muttered, "Show some respect."

"Man, it's good to be outside," Walken said as they walked to Doug's car. "My apartment's too small. It's like a prison cell. I need a bigger place. I need a better job. Working at a gas station—"

"That thing at the bank didn't work out?" Doug asked.

"Nah. Mr. Kirby said they need someone with some experience and a degree. I remember how he used to come into the locker room after all our games and tell me I reminded him of Pete Maravich. He was the biggest jersey-sniffer of them all! Now he won't give me a job. I told him most people in this town remember me. I'd be good for business."

"What did Kirby say to that?" Doug asked.

"He said it's been a long time since I was a player. Maybe he's right. But that little hot dog Granger woulda never broken my scoring record last year without launching at least ten three-pointers a game." He snorted. "Out there at the top of the key, where nobody guarded him. I earned my points, man. Posting guards up on the low block. Slashing through the lane, guys hanging on my arm. If I wanted to make my living from out there in deep downtown, I coulda. I could drain those shots in my sleep. And when I did shoot from deep downtown, I did it out there from NBA range. That way, I could prove I could really shoot and draw the defense out to boot."

"Yeah," Doug said, nodding toward Cody and Pork Chop. "Rock had a good outside shot, but he didn't stand out there launching missiles, that's for sure."

"Yeah, you can't get the other team in foul trouble that way. You can't force the action. And don't get me started on zone defenses. That's all anybody plays anymore. Nobody has the stuff to play man-to-man, the way it used to be. You know what that pretty-boy Granger told me? He said that on the nights before games, he used to pray for a zone defense. That's just like him—pray for an easy way out."

The quartet entered the Dairy Delight. Fred Betts, the assistant manager, gave them a puzzled smile and said, "Back so soon?"

"It's Rock's birthday, so we're treating him to lunch," Doug explained.

"Dude, my birthday's next month," Walken whispered too loudly.

"So we're early," Doug said. "Sue me."

Betts took their orders—a cheeseburger and a mug of root beer for Walken, nothing for Cody and Doug, and a medium order of "dessert French fries" for Pork Chop—and turned away.

"You know," Walken observed, "Betts got kinda fat, too. He's got a table muscle, just like me. But look at all that hair. It's not fair. You know, I never wore a baseball cap, because my old man said it would make me bald like him. He said that sunlight and air were good for your scalp and all. But now I'm twenty-six, my head's getting shiny, and I've got hair growing in places that have never even seen the light of day!"

"I know what you should do," Doug advised. "Start wearing your underwear on your head."

"Ha!" Walken croaked. He gulped down his root beer and stared at the empty mug. His eyes followed a frothy cloud of foam as it slid to the bottom of the glass. He rose awkwardly and walked to the jukebox. Doug and Cody followed. Pork Chop stayed in the booth, enjoying his fries.

"What's with music now, fellas?" Walken asked. "Rap. Hip-hop. All that stuff. What's up with that? It's like someone yellin' at you for six minutes. And don't get me started on these boy bands!"

Doug laughed. "I hear that. But don't let my little brother hear you dissin' rap."

"Whatever." Walken scanned the choices. "I wouldn't pay a quarter for any of this stuff. Whatever happened to The Who? Where are the Stones on this stupid machine? Music has really gone to the dogs."

Then Walken stopped. "Hey, I think Fred's talkin' about me to that customer! Listen!"

"I'm telling you, he was great!" they heard Betts whisper loudly to a newly arrived patron. "He had the smoothest jumper you ever saw. He was quick, too. And ballhandling? His hands were like magic."

"He don't look like much now. Looks like a waste-product," the customer countered.

"He was great. The best this town's ever seen. He scored thirty-seven against Holy Name one year."

"So? That Granger boy scored forty this year, and he's only a junior."

Doug awkwardly put his arm around Walken's shoulder. "Don't worry about it, Rock. You were the best. Anyone who knows basketball knows that."

"That's right," Walken sniffed. "I mean, you've seen that Granger kid play. He's a gunner. A hot dog. And he's not fundamentally sound."

Doug sighed. "I don't think the new coach really teaches the fundamentals."

Walken shook his head and exhaled sadly. "Whatever. I just can't believe that Betts forgot it was thirty-eight points. And it wasn't against Holy Name, to boot! It was Saint Stephen's! He kept the stats, for Pete's sake. And it was on the front page of the *Grant Gazette*. I even got written up in the Springs paper. Nobody came close to that record until this year. What's wrong with Betts? Maybe he's going senile prematurely, just like I'm goin' bald."

"Let's get out of here," Doug urged. "Hey, you wanna go over to the park and school these two eighth graders?"

Walken tried to make himself look taller as they headed for the exit. Cody saw him crane his neck and pull in his stomach. "Later, Betts," Walken called.

They stepped outside. Walken squinted. "Man, it's too bright out here."

They returned to the apartment, where—after fifteen minutes—they abandoned their basketball plans. Walken couldn't find his ball.

"I coulda sworn it was in this closet," he said. "But I haven't played in a long, long time."

"Dude, I can't believe that was Rock Walken," Pork Chop said, breaking a long silence in Doug's Camry. "He doesn't look anything like his pics at the school. Are you sure he's only twenty-six? He could be forty. Man, he looks old!"

"Yeah," Doug said, his voice laced with sadness. "They call him Dead Man Walken behind his back. I watched him play since he was in junior high. Even then there was buzz about him. I remember high school players coming down to the middle school to watch him. He was one of the best natural athletes I've ever seen. Definitely the best to ever come out of this town."

"Come on," Cody argued, "better than you, Doug?"

"Way better. He's only six-two, and he could dunk with two hands. He dunked as a freshman, Code. And he was probably only five-eleven then. He ran a four-four forty. He was a wide receiver like you. If he ever caught the ball in the open field, it was game over."

Pork Chop belched thoughtfully. "I don't get it—if he was such a rock-star athlete, what happened to him?"

"He went to college and majored in football. Sound familiar, little brother? He didn't study. He didn't go to class. He just partied a lot and hoped his talent would carry him. It didn't."

"But—"

"But what, Chop? Check this out—I'm majoring in education, not football. I'm going to be a teacher. Maybe coach a little. But I'm not sure about that. If I coach too many knuckleheads like you, I might get an ulcer."

"But what about your game, big dawg?" Pork Chop protested. "You've got skills, you've got strength. You always said you were gonna go pro—what got into you?"

"Common sense, dude. And I haven't bragged about going pro since I was sixteen, at least. Look, Chop, I spent the last two summers working out with college players. It was a reality check for me, bigtime. I can't believe how many guys are bigger, stronger, and faster than I am. Besides, I'm more proud of my 3.8 GPA than I am of any my athletic accomplishments."

"But you gained over a thousand yards this past season."

"Yeah, I can run over anybody in our league. For that matter, I can outrun most of the linebackers around here. But that won't happen at the next level. You don't plow over a two-hundred-and-thirty-pound linebacker who's all muscle. You don't trample a three-hundred-pound defensive tackle—even if he's *not* all muscle. The simple fact is that I can't play fullback in college. I couldn't hit the holes quick enough, and I'd never be able to turn the corner on linebackers or defensive ends from Wisconsin or Ohio State."

Pork Chop pressed his palms over his ears. "I'm not hearin' any of this. I think my milk shake froze your brain, yo. You're trippin'!"

Doug pounded the steering wheel. "No, Chop, you're trippin'. You know how many guys our league has sent to the pros in its history? Zero."

Cody whistled through his teeth. "But this league has been around for, like, forty years."

"More like fifty," Doug said firmly. "Guys, I have collected the All-America football rosters since I was

a kid. The premium high school players in the country. And only a few of them really make a name for
themselves in college. Even fewer than that have any
kind of pro career. There have even been Heisman
Trophy winners who never made it in the pros. You
guys ever hear of Gino Torretta?"

Pork Chop and Cody looked at each other. "Nah,"
Cody said.

"Well, he won the Heisman several years ago.
Voted the best college player in the land. He didn't
play a lick in the NFL."

Cody eyed Pork Chop, who looked to be on the
verge of either crying or vomiting. "But, Doug," Cody
said, hoping to coax a response that would help his
friend feel better, "don't you still dream about playing
in the NFL, even if you don't talk about it anymore?"

"Sure, little man. And I'm not saying that I won't
work hard to be a good college player. And, after that,
who knows? I might try out for the pros, maybe make
a preseason roster. Or do some arena-league stuff for
a year or two. Just to say I played pro ball. But teach-
ing is my long-term goal. If I'm going to spend hours
a day preparing for something, it's not gonna be a
game—even a great game like football. Look, Code,
the average NFL career is only a few years. You have
peanut butter in your kitchen cupboard that has a

longer shelf life than an NFL player. And what happens after that? I'll tell you what happens: The rest of your life. That's what I'm preparing for, right now."

Pork Chop leaned forward in his seat, resting his face in his hands. Doug reached over and patted his brother on the back. "And, if college ball ever gets in the way of my education, I'm hanging up my pads for good."

"I think I'm gonna be sick," Pork Chop muttered.

"I think I'm gonna be one terrific teacher," Doug said proudly.

"Come on," Coach Clayton said, walking among the sprawled bodies on the infield grass, "this is the last hard practice before our first meet. Let's make it a good one. You guys act like you're about ready to die. Ha! Eight quarters is nothing."

"Easy for him to say," Goddard gasped.

"Yeah," Cody agreed, rolling from his back to a sitting position. "But at least we're almost done. Only two more."

As Cody and Goddard struggled to their feet, Alston whipped by on the track, sprinting the straightaway. "Be a sprinter—have the time of your life!" he taunted, before slowing to a jog.

"I hate him," Goddard said. "He thinks he's such a rock star."

"He's all right," Cody said.

"Since when? He's a loudmouth and a hot dog."

"Maybe not so much anymore. And I think he was just having fun with us. He wasn't doggin' us."

"I can't believe you've had a change of heart about Alston! What about how he was always dissin' you in basketball?"

"Goddard, don't you remember what happened at the end of basketball season—how he apologized to the team? How he gave it all he had in the championship game? Maybe it's not *my* heart that's changing."

"Goddard! Martin!" Coach Clayton barked. "Is your little gabfest over? If so, I'd like both of you to give me an eighty-second quarter, if you don't mind."

Cody and Goddard jogged to the start line. Drew was already there, inhaling deeply and staring down the track. The rest of the distance men filled in the spaces beside and behind him.

"You don't want to get in front of Drew Phelps— unless you liked being shoved into the infield grass or having your calves stepped on," Cody had explained to newcomers on the first day of intervals.

Cody smiled as he heard Coach Clayton yell, "Set —bang!" and start the runners. Drew sprinted ahead of the pack, hugging the first turn. When he hit the first straightaway, he lengthened his stride and shook out his arms.

Cody tried to keep within ten yards of Drew, but as they hit the second turn, he felt a sharp pain in his right side. *I don't know why they call it "side stitch,"* he thought. *It oughta be "side stab." Because I feel like Zorro or one of the Three Musketeers just ran me through with a sword!*

He dragged himself across the line as Coach Clayton barked, "Eighty-two, eighty-three, eighty-four. A little slow there, Martin. You gotta concentrate on what you're doing. You gotta hold your form, hold your rhythm. There's more to running track than just alternating feet and turning left every now and again."

Cody nodded and staggered to the infield to find a spit-free place to collapse. Coach Clayton turned his attention to Goddard, who was approaching the finish line.

"January, February, March," Coach called derisively. "What are you doing, Mr. Goddard—looking for a contact lens? This is track practice, my man, not a charity walkathon. Save the whales on your own time!"

Goddard gave the coach a wounded look.

"Aw, for Pete's sake, Goddard. I'm just woofin' ya," Coach Clayton said. "You know I admire your guts.

But it wouldn't kill ya to try to pick up the pace just a little, that's all I'm sayin'."

Cody had just begun to slump down on the long jump runway when he felt two bony hands under his armpits.

"No, Code," Drew said as he lifted him to his feet.

"Aw, Phelps," Cody groaned. "Don't give me that 'you gotta keep moving' speech again. I need to rest. I'm whupped."

"You might cramp up," Drew countered. "And it's better for your breathing if you stay upright. Besides, you need to train your brain and your body that you can keep moving, even when you're dead tired. Don't give in to exhaustion. Don't give in to pain—ever."

Drew's eyes were penetrating, intense. "You give in once," he said, "and it starts getting easier to do it again. So when that urge comes, you gotta squash it. Like a cockroach."

I'd like to squash you, Cody thought, but he nodded instead.

"We have just one more," Drew said, walking beside Cody now. "Let's really bust it, okay? It'll make coach happy. Besides, you want to impress your dad, don't you?"

Cody felt his mouth pop open. "My dad?"

"Yeah," Drew said, pointing, "isn't that him by the pole vault pit, talking to Robyn and Pork Chop?"

Okay, there's no possible way this turns out good, Cody reasoned. *Best-case scenario—let me see. I just get embarrassed. Worst case? I get humiliated. I have to move to another land. A faraway, distant land.*

"All right," he heard Coach Clayton yell. "One more. Let's try to get everybody under eighty this time. It won't kill ya. I haven't had a distance man die on me yet."

Cody saw his dad put his hand on Robyn's head, as if he were trying to bless her. *I wouldn't mind too much if this did kill me,* he thought.

On Coach Clayton's command, Drew charged ahead and took his customary place at the head of the pack. Cody tucked in behind him, hoping to protect himself from the stiff wind that had picked up on the backstretch during the previous four-hundred.

But, as they came out of the first turn, Drew had opened up a four-stride lead on Cody.

Cody willed himself forward, closing the gap. Drew spun his head over his right shoulder. "Good, Code," he said, his voice even and strong. "Stay right on my afterburners, and I'll break the wind for you down the backstretch. But when we get to the homestretch, you're on your own. I need to finish this one in seventy-five, at least."

A gaspy "Okay," was all Cody could manage in response.

As Cody entered the final 75 yards of the interval, he heard his dad chirp, "Okay, buddy, let's go! Kick it in! You can do it!"

Oh, please, somebody kill me now, Cody complained to himself. *My dad, in his business suit, just called me "buddy," in front of God and everybody. He's cheering for me—at practice! This pretty much ensures my getting voted Most Uncool Kid in the history of junior high athletics.*

Cody crossed the finish line as Coach Clayton barked, "Seventy-nine! Whoa, baby! For the love of Kip Keino, that's the way to finish strong, Cody Martin!"

Cody staggered to the pole vault pit and flung himself on the apple-red padding. *If Phelps comes over here and tells me to "get up and walk it off,"* he thought, *he's gonna get a size eight-and-a-half Adidas down his throat.*

But it was Cody's dad, flanked by Robyn and Pork Chop, who appeared first, his dad beaming down at him with that goofy parental smile that made Cody wish he were a turtle, so he could tuck his head inside his shell until it was safe to show his face again.

"Good running, Son. Only one guy beat you, and he's mighty swift! Is he new?"

"No, Dad. That's Drew Phelps. He won every race last year. You only came to one meet, so you may not remember him."

"Well, he's mighty swift, in any case."

Oh no, Cody shuddered, *did my dad just say "mighty swift" again?*

He sat up. He felt the urge to spit, but he couldn't do that with Robyn and his dad there. *I could spit if it was just Pork Chop*, he said to himself. *I could spit on Chop's shoe and he wouldn't care.*

Dad was talking again, and Cody snapped to attention when he heard the word "dandy."

"Dandy running, Cody. Just dandy."

Just breathe, Cody told himself. *You can get through this. You've already lived through "mighty swift" and "dandy." It can't get much worse.*

"Thanks, Dad," he said, hoping to prevent a possible "okey-dokey" or "willy-nilly," "but it was only practice. We're just trying to get to the point where we can hit our quarters consistently. Drew, he hit all of his in seventy-five or less. Sub-five pace."

His father flashed a toothy smile. "Wow, that's—"

"Dandy?" Pork Chop offered.

"Indeed!" Cody's dad concurred.

Cody slit his eyes and glared at Pork Chop, who responded by mouthing the words "Super-duper neato!"

"So," Robyn said, "how did you do, Cody? Were you consistent?"

"Aw, I lost my focus on two of 'em, but the rest were within three or four seconds of my goal. You sprinters gonna be tough again this year?"

"Not bad. Janet's got a bad hammy. Jessica got fat over the winter. Other than that, we're good."

"Excuse me, Robyn," Cody's father asked, his forehead crinkling, "did you make reference to a girl named Janet's 'ammy'? What, pray tell, is an ammy?"

Robyn giggled. "No, sir, I said *hammy*. Hamstring, you know. Janet pulled hers a while ago, and it's been slow to heal."

"Gosh, I hope she recuperates soon."

"She'd better. Our relay teams will be hurtin' without her. She's the anchor leg."

Cody's dad nodded. "When is your first competition?"

"Our first competition is this weekend," Pork Chop said, lacing the word "competition" with a bit of faux British flair. "It's the Taylor Invitational. You coming, sir?"

"We'll have to see, Deke. Work is quite hectic right now."

"But the meet's on Saturday, sir," Pork Chop noted.

"Yes, but the paper comes out every day. And that means I often have to work every day."

"That stinks," Robyn said.

Cody felt like saying, "Amen!" but he swallowed the word before it escaped his lips. *You don't know the half of it*, he thought.

"So, Dad," he said, trying to sound cheerful, "what brings you to practice?"

His father smiled sheepishly. "Well, Son, I came to take you home for dinner. A real home-cooked dinner!"

Cody scratched his head. "At our home, you mean?"

"Yeppers!"

"Did one of the ladies from church bring something over?"

"Nope!" His father smiled.

"But, Dad," Cody began tentatively, "you can't cook. I mean, you haven't tried to make even one of the recipes in the cookbook I gave you for Christmas."

His dad looked wounded. "I know, but I will, in due time. But for tonight I made, shall we say, other arrangements."

Cody looked to Pork Chop for help.

"Don't gawk at me, dawg. I'm in the dark here myself," his best friend muttered.

Before anyone could respond, Pork Chop released a bark of laughter as he looked at his caramel-skinned arms. "Hey, 'in the dark'—I just kinda made a joke!"

Cody rolled his eyes. "If that's what you want to call it."

Pork Chop clapped his friend sharply on the back. "Whatever, bro. Why don't you go home now and eat your 'other arrangements.' Nice to see you again, Mr. Martin. Way to run, Robyn. And, Code, good practice, dawg!"

Robyn smiled at him. "Yeah, good practice, dawg!" She raised her right hand and waved her fingers at Cody's father. "Nice to see you, sir. God bless."

"I'll meet you at the car, Dad," Cody said, breaking into a trot. *I gotta get out of here,* he thought, *before things get even more weird and embarrassing.*

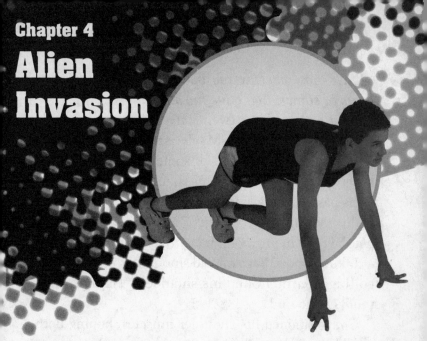

Chapter 4
Alien Invasion

The somewhat-cute woman with coal-black hair moved toward Cody, tentatively, but with a smile.

She looks like she's either gonna try to hug me, he surmised, *or else she's one of those lady wrestlers and she's closin' in to give me a pile driver!*

"Hi!" she said, in a voice that was too loud for the cramped Martin living room. She was using what his mom would have called her "outdoor voice." "I'm Beth. I've heard so much about you, and I'm glad to finally meet you!"

Finally? Cody thought as Beth entered his personal space. The perfume she was wearing was too strong and too sweet. Not subtle, the way Mom's had been.

What—has meeting me been one of your lifelong goals or something? Give me a break!

Beth looked about twenty-five. She was definitely not from the church. Maybe she was from Dad's work—one of his interns or something. She held her arms out to him, grasping his shoulders. Cody kept his arms pasted to his sides. He tried to send Beth a telepathic message—*If you think I'm huggin' some strange chick in my living room, you are seriously dreaming.*

Like a dancer, Beth moved smoothly to Cody's side, coiling an arm around his shoulder. "Hard practice today?" she said.

Cody stiffened his shoulder muscles, hoping Beth would get the hint. She must have, because she released her grip on him and let her arm slip to her side, where it belonged.

"Uh, yeah, practice was pretty hard. But in a good way, though. Know what I mean?"

"Yeah. I ran track in high school. College, too."

"No foolin'. What event?"

"Events, actually," Beth said, still smiling. "The four hundred and eight hundred. And a relay here and there."

I'd love to know how fast you ran, he thought. *But just in case you're faster than I am—* "Track's not really my sport," he said quickly. "I do it mainly to stay in shape for other sports. But I've kinda gotten into distance running."

"You have the build for it."

"You mean I'm skinny."

"I mean you're lean and strong. I can tell you're an athlete."

Cody studied Beth. They were about the same height. He recalled how he used to look over the top of his mom's head whenever she confronted him about some misdeed—and how she always busted him for it.

"You look me in the eyes when I'm talking to you, Cody Martin," she'd say. "Don't try to stare over me. What, are you looking over yonder for the cavalry to come to your rescue? That ain't happening."

He dropped his gaze from Beth's face to his shoes. He felt the simultaneous urge to throw up, cry, and run as fast as he could until he passed out.

"Dinner's almost ready," Beth said, as she turned her back on him and walked toward the kitchen. "You best get washed up."

He waited for his dad to enter the house. One thought echoed in his head—*Luke Martin, you got some explaining to do.* He heard the garage door close, and then his dad enter the kitchen. He heard him say, "Beth, that smells divine!" Then there was a sound. It could have been a kiss. But it also could have been a

Tupperware container opening, or the sound of bacon popping in a fry pan.

Now his father was in the living room. Cody looked at him and shrugged, palms up.

"Later," his dad whispered firmly. "For now, get upstairs and get showered. Quickly. You don't smell all that good."

"Yeah?" Cody muttered as he bounded up the stairs two at a time. "Well, at least I don't smell like I spent all day marinating in Chanel Number Five, or whatever that stuff is. At least I'm not the stinkin' perfumigator!"

He dove onto his bed, grabbed the phone receiver, and hit the first number on speed dial.

"Porter residence," a gravel-coated voice informed him.

"Is Deke in, please?"

"Nah," Pork Chop's father chuckled good-naturedly. "He and that no-account, economy-sized big brother of his are still in town, probably eating everything in sight."

"Oh."

"Is that you, Cody Martin?"

"Yes, Mr. Porter. Yes sir."

"I thought so. It's good to hear your voice. How you doin', Son?"

Cody swallowed hard at the question. He knew exactly what Pork Chop's father meant. "I'm okay, sir. It's still hard, you know? Thank you for asking. Not many people do that anymore."

Mr. Porter chuckled sadly. "Yeah. Well, I send one up for you every night—you and your father."

"Thanks. We need all the prayer we can get."

"Son, we *all* need all the prayer we can get. I tell Deke to pray for you, too, but he's not much of a prayer, being the no-account heathen that he is. But he sure does like that Pod record you got him for Christmas. Plays it all the time."

Cody crinkled his nose. "Pod, sir? I think I'm confused here."

"Ain't that the name of that group—Pod?"

"Oh, you mean P.O.D. Yeah, that's the disc I got him for Christmas."

"P.O.D., huh? I get it. It's one of them anachronisms."

Cody smiled. "That's about the size of it, sir."

"Them P.O.D. fellers must be Christians, as best as I can make out from the lyrics. Albeit, I can make out only half of what they're sayin'."

"Yes sir, I believe they are."

"Well, that's dandy. Maybe they'll do old Pork Chop some good."

"That's why I bought it for him, sir."

"You're a good man, Cody Martin. I'll have Deke call you when he gets in."

"Thank you, sir. And thank you for your prayers. It means a lot to me."

Several silent seconds passed. Cody thought the line might have gone dead. He heard a deep sigh and then, "Oh, my. Okay. Well, I gotta run. May God bless you, Cody."

Cody returned the receiver to the charger and stared at the ceiling. Was crusty old Mr. Porter actually crying? He couldn't be sure, but there was something in his voice.

"Soup's on, buddy!" he heard his dad call in an overly cheerful voice.

"Uh-oh," Cody muttered. "No time to shower."

He rushed to the bathroom, whipped off his T-shirt, and began scrubbing his torso with the damp washcloth he had conveniently left balled up in his sink that morning.

This should take care of at least the major stinkage, he thought. *And now for the insurance.*

He opened his medicine cabinet and grabbed his deodorant. He applied a thick coat under both arms and then ran it over his chest and stomach too.

"Cody!" Dad's voice had lost its cheer this time.

He returned to his bedroom and frantically grabbed shirts from the pyre-shaped mound in the middle of the floor, sniffing them to find a clean one.

After rejecting six shirts on the basis of stains, smell, or both, he found one from basketball camp that met his approval. He wriggled into it as he stutter-stepped quickly down the stairs.

Dad and Beth were sitting beside each other on one side of the dining room table, which was covered, for the first time since his mom's funeral, with a white tablecloth. Cody could see the deep creases where it had been folded.

It looks like a topographical map of the Sahara Desert or something, not a tablecloth, he thought.

Cody took his place opposite Beth and his father. "Dinner sure smells good," he offered, hoping his words didn't sound as hollow and insincere to his audience as they did to him.

"Thank you, Cody," Beth said, bowing her head to accept the compliment. "It's spaghetti. Your mom's recipe. I know I can't cook as well as she does—uh, did. Anyway, I just, um, hope you like it."

He frowned. *I was going to try to like it, until you said what you just said.*

Now Beth was yammering about tossed salad and French bread, but it was mostly noise to Cody. He felt pressure building in his head, like it was a balloon someone was inflating—overinflating.

He smiled and nodded at Beth, who had moved on to pontificating about extra-virgin olive oil and how it differed from regular olive oil. She snaked her arm around his dad's back as she talked. He leaned against her and smiled. It was all Cody could do to hold his tears back.

She's not an intern from work, he reasoned. *They haven't talked about Dad's job once. She's not a private chef he hired just so I could enjoy some home cooking. She's touching my dad, and he keeps giving her that goofy, smiley-bear face he used to give Mom. I wish this were a TV show. Then I could push my chair away from the table, stand, and ask politely, "May I be excused?" Then I could retreat to my room and bury my head in my pillow and cry. Then Dad would follow me upstairs, sit on my bed, and put a hand on my shoulder. He would speak quietly and tell me how sorry he was for being so insensitive.*

But this isn't TV. This is real life, and in real life you have to sit up and face the spaghetti. Because, even though this whole thing stinks, Dad is smiling, smiling like a jack-o'-lantern, and I haven't seen him smile like that in almost a year. He's happy, and I can't do anything to mess that up.

Cody chased down a mouthful of spaghetti with a large gulp of water. For a moment he thought the whole mess was going to stick in his throat. He waited. *Come on, gravity, do your stuff,* he urged. *If*

Dad has to come over here and Heimlich me in front of his new woman, he'll never forgive me.

He went to the water glass again. Mercifully, he felt the food sliding down toward its proper destination.

"Thanks for the great meal," he said, dabbing his mouth with a cloth napkin. He tried to inject his voice with as much happiness as he could, without sounding fake.

Sometimes, when she was in a cynical mood, his mom would quote her high school drama teacher, "Sincerity is the key to success, on the stage and in real life. If you can learn to fake sincerity, you've got it made."

Cody assumed he was doing a good job of faking sincerity, because he made it through dinner without drawing any disapproving glares from his dad. And he even made Beth giggle when he told the story of how Pork Chop wore his T-shirt inside out to the homecoming dance. When Cody asked him why, Chop explained matter-of-factly, "This is the clean side."

When Dad and his date retreated to the kitchen, Cody slipped quietly upstairs, picked up the phone, and called his youth pastor.

"Thank heaven you're there, Blake," Cody said. "I have to talk."

"What's up, Code?"

"Well, my dad is downstairs right now with a girl—as in girlfriend. Her name is Beth."

"Whoa, wait a minute—are you sure she's not just a friend from work?"

"Yeah, Blake. We get cable TV here. I know what's what. Besides, they were talking about movies they've seen, restaurants they've eaten at. I thought Dad was just putting in tons of overtime at the paper, but I guess his job isn't the only thing he's been workin'. And check this—she's only about your age! She looks like she could be my older sister, but she might turn out to be my, uh—man, I can't even say it."

"Cody, I can hear that you're upset, but let's not get ahead of ourselves here. Just because he brought someone home to meet you doesn't mean they're going to marry. A few dates don't equal marriage. Lots of dates don't even equal marriage. You're talkin' to a guy who knows. Remember, I have two—count 'em, two—broken engagements on my resume. They both decided I wasn't the guy they wanted to marry. And they were right. God always has our best interests at heart. Now that I'm older, I know that when the right woman comes along, the Lord will let me know."

"I know, B, but you should see the way he looks at her. I know that look. I used to see it all the time."

"Code, I know this is rough on you, and I'm sorry. But, please, realize that it's been almost a year. And I know your dad a bit. He's not cut out to be alone."

"Alone? What about me? What am I, invisible?"

"Come on, dude. You're fourteen. And, as you said, you have cable. You know what I mean."

"I guess I do. But, still, this just can't happen. At least not now. I'll totally trip out if he ends up marrying her. He can't bring some stranger into our house and start calling her 'honey,' 'babe,' and all those names he used to call Mom. And he better not expect me to call Beth 'Mom.' No way is that going to happen!"

"Cody, I don't know that your dad would expect that of you, if this relationship goes that way. *If.* That's one of the biggest little words in the English language."

"Well, this is one 'if' that better not turn out to be 'when.'"

Cody heard Blake sigh deeply. "Dude, we went through 1 Corinthians 13 earlier in the school year. Remember the part that says, 'Love does not demand its own way'?"

"Yeah," Cody confessed.

"Well? What are you doing right now over this thing?"

"I feel what you're saying, B. But I can't do this. I just about blew chow during dinner, watching the two of them."

"Fortunately, you don't have to do this alone. Fortunately, you can rely on God for wisdom, strength, support. And you have friends. Good friends. And a youth pastor who cares about you. A dad, too. I believe he'll take your feelings into account. He'll talk to you if things start getting really serious."

"You sure about that?"

"Pretty sure. Especially since I'll have Pastor Taylor call and check up on him—maybe invite him in for a counseling session or two."

"Thanks, B. I appreciate what you're trying to do. I have to be honest, though. I hope this thing with Dad and Beth goes nowhere. That's what I'm going to pray."

"You could do that. Or you could pray that God's will be done—not Cody Martin's."

"But if they get married, my life will be a mess."

"Cody, listen to me. I have two broken engagements that still hurt, long after they happened. I have a sister who's wrecking her life and won't let me help. I got fired from my first church job. Two years and it still hangs over me like a storm cloud."

"Whoa—I didn't know all that, B. That's messy."

"Life is messy sometimes. Mine is a tangled mess right now. I used to pray that God would untangle all the gnarly knots. Some of them he did untangle.

Others are still here. But God's given me the grace to live with the knots. Maybe that should be your prayer."

"Okay, Blake," Cody said quietly, "it will be."

"Hey, is Beth still there?"

"Yeah. I hear 'em laughing down there."

"Maybe you could go downstairs and say good night. Be a gracious host. Do it for your dad."

"I will. Thanks, B. This helps. You know, you should be a youth pastor or something."

Blake laughed. "I'll keep that in mind. Now, get down there and do some good. I'll be praying for you."

Chapter 5

Track Meet, or Dead Meat?

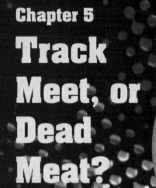

Cody sat by Drew in the track infield, stretching his left hamstring. He studied his friend, lying on his stomach beside him, not even breathing hard, although he was only five minutes removed from destroying the Taylor Invitational field in the 1600. He ran a 5.12, easing up on the last half-lap, at his coach's command.

"You got this one in the bag, Flash," the coach had said as Drew whipped by him. "Save some gas for the two-mile."

Cody shook his head. "Dude, I'd say you're in midseason form already. That Mack dude couldn't hang with you after the first lap. And even though you shut it down at the end, he still didn't gain on you."

Drew rolled to his back and stared at the sky. "Yeah, but Cabrera will be in the two-mile, and he's tough."

"Well, do me a favor," Cody said. "Get him good and winded early. Work him so hard that he can't talk smack to me like he did in hoops. Man, I hate playing basketball against that guy. He thinks it's a full-contact sport."

"Isn't it?"

"I guess. The way he and Pork Chop play it, it is. But with Cabrera, it's more than just the contact that goes with the territory. He's a cheap shot artist."

"Well, watch him on the track then," Drew advised. "He might try to throw an elbow or spike you."

"Or you," Cody said.

"He isn't fast enough to get me."

"I thought you said he's tough in the two."

"He is," Drew said. "But not tough enough. Especially now that you've given me some extra motivation."

Cody stood and headed for the shot put area. He arrived in time to see Pork Chop unleash a forty-two foot throw, accompanied by a gorilla-like grunt loud enough to make several girls from Central Middle School giggle, with their hands over their mouths.

Pork Chop joined Cody in the crowd as Miller from Central moved to the ring to compete. "Everybody might as well go home, Code," Pork Chop said. "I feel strong, like a bull."

Miller scratched on his throw, and the contingent of Central girls headed for the track. As they passed Cody and Pork Chop, the latter flexed his right bicep and asked, "Hey, girls, wanna feel my muscle?"

They giggled some more and began running to the track, looking back at Pork Chop at least five times along the way.

"Chop, you can stop posing now. They're long gone. Probably want to watch Antwan Clay run the hundred."

Pork Chop began working his right arm in slow, wide circles. "Yeah, you're probably right. But Alston will whip him, just like last year. Besides, they're watching Clay just out of school loyalty. They love me."

"Probably not as much as you love yourself. Why are you in such a good mood, anyway?"

"Because, dude, it's spring. It's track season. Nobody face-masking me or trying to leg-whip me on the football field. Nobody hacking me across the face while I'm going for a layup. All I gotta do is fling a couple of round objects, collect two gold medals, cheer you on in the two-mile, then get on the bus and nap all the way back to Grant. And look—the sun is out and there's not a cloud around. I might even improve my tan. Hey, by the end of the season, I might be as dark as Dylan."

"Well, I'm glad you're enjoying the day. Because I'm so nervous I can't sit still. Two miles! That's a long time to run full out. I'm afraid I'm gonna get smoked. Phelps will probably lap me. Maybe Cabrera, too. That would stink."

Pork Chop arched an eyebrow and grinned. "Want me to trip Cabrera? Or maybe accidentally hit him with a discus?"

"Thanks for the offer. But I gotta take my medicine. Just do me a favor. Don't watch. It's gonna be ugly."

"I'm gonna watch, dawg," Chop said. "And I'll cheer for you no matter where you finish. Just relax, okay? I know you've been putting in a lot of miles. And just hanging out with Phelps all the time has got to help you. Maybe some of his mojo has rubbed off on you."

"We'll see," Cody mumbled as he headed for his fourth visit to the rest room.

The sun was low in the sky when Cody heard the final call for the boys' 3200-meter run. The Grant boys were in second place, well behind Central, but comfortably ahead of East.

Still, there was considerable buzz surrounding the race. The meet record of 11.30 was sure to fall—the question was, by how much. And who would break it? Everyone remembered how Drew Phelps had dominated the 1600 and 800 as a seventh grader. But seventh graders weren't allowed to compete in the 3200, so this was uncharted territory.

In fact, Drew had never competed in this distance in his life. Opposing coaches wondered if he had the stamina for the longer race. Cabrera already had a 3200 under his belt. He had run an 11.36 at a dual meet the week before. He was in top shape, having competed in football and basketball. Drew, on the other hand, sat out cross-country season with plantar fasciitis, and he hadn't even bothered to go out for basketball.

Cody stood directly behind Drew at the starting line. It was a small field, only fourteen runners. *Great*, Cody thought, *nowhere to hide if I run out of gas*.

Cabrera was next to Drew, springing up and down to stay loose and warm. He looked tough. His quad muscles looked like loaves of brown bread, and his ever-present sneer was more confident than ever.

Drew alternated shaking his legs out, stealing a quick glance at Cabrera. He turned to Cody and whispered, "Run an even pace. Don't get caught up in the buzz of the start. I'm gonna take Cabrera out fast. Punish him. It's gonna mess up my splits, but it'll put him in pain early. And two miles is a long way to run when you're hurtin'. So just stay back and run your race. If you run eight, eighty-nine-second laps, you'll turn in an 11.52. That'll probably place today."

Cody nodded. Drew spun around as the starter yelled, "Gentlemen, I'll give you the command to set and then you'll hear the gun. You must have a stride and a-half to cut in front of someone. And, late in the race, if you are about to be lapped, we'll have people along the track to tell you to move to an outside lane, so the faster runner can get by you."

Hey, thanks for reminding me about the prospect of getting lapped, Cody moaned inwardly. *My stomach had just stopped churning—thanks for getting it goin' again.*

Even with the prefatory "Set," the gun startled Cody when its loud report bounced off his eardrums. The pack was off, in a flurry of clicking spikes and scuffing racing flats. Cody felt himself being pushed from behind. He panicked, as he feared stepping on Drew in front of him.

He needn't have worried. Drew rocketed ahead, as if he were running one of the sprints, not the longest race of the meet. Cabrera followed on his right shoulder. Cody saw the East runner jab Drew in the side with his left elbow. Drew didn't acknowledge the attack, but Cody knew it had to hurt. He found himself accelerating toward the lead twosome.

Midway through the first lap, their lead on him had shrunk from ten yards to only five. Cody pondered what he could do to Cabrera when he caught him. Maybe step on his heel. Or at least tell him Pork Chop was waiting to ambush him behind the high jump pit.

Cody willed his legs to turn faster. He had to catch Cabrera. Drew needed help. But as he headed into the straightaway to complete his first lap, he had lost two yards on the duo.

Moments later, as Drew and Cabrera completed their first lap, Cody panicked as he heard one of the Taylor assistant coaches call out the splits: "Seventy-five, seventy-six, seventy-seven—"

Seventy-five seconds for the first lap? Cody hoped he had heard wrong. That's five-minute-mile pace. *I know Drew said he was gonna punish Cabrera, but this is ridiculous. There's nobody on the high school team who can keep this kind of pace for two miles.*

Cody hit lap one in seventy-nine seconds. *A little hot,* he thought. *But not too bad. Besides, I feel good. Those guys are still only about ten yards ahead. Maybe I'll close the gap this lap. Who knows? Maybe all those miles with Drew are paying off!*

Cody was still running strong halfway through lap two. He focused on his form. Smooth arm swing. Sure, quick strides. Keeping his upper body straight up, not leaning forward or slouching.

It wasn't until he rounded the second turn of the lap that the bear got him.

Cody had heard many tales of the bear, especially from Gage and the other 400-meter guys. Even Robyn had met the bear a time or two.

The bear was clever, devious. He left you alone for the first part of your race. You began to think he was just an urban legend, like the vanishing hitchhiker or the guy with a hook for a hand. But then, when you least expected him, he jumped on your back. He clawed at your throat, cutting off your wind. He pummeled your stomach until it ached and throbbed. And he was heavy, so very heavy. It felt as if his sheer bulk would drive you to the ground.

The bear threatened to take Cody down, and he still had more than a mile and a-half to go in the race. He staggered through lap two in 2.49. *Great,* he thought, *second lap eleven seconds slower than the first. What was that Drew said about running an even pace? I can't believe I didn't listen to him. He's gonna kill me—if I live through this, that is.*

To try to take his mind off the pain, Cody scanned the track to see how Drew's strategy was working on Cabrera. From the backstretch, he saw them, now almost a quarter lap ahead. Cabrera was still on Drew like a shadow. Cody wondered if the bear was going to get Drew, too. After all, he went out faster than anybody.

Drew and Cabrera had about 250 meters on Cody when they hit the halfway mark. Cody glanced at his chronograph watch—5.32. They had let up a bit, but they were still running crazy. If they didn't fall apart, they'd both destroy the old meet record. Grant's school record was toast, too. It was only 11.38.

Cody shook his head as Mack and another runner from Holy Family passed him. He was now in fifth place. The top six guys earned points, and fourth through sixth got ribbons. He had never earned a ribbon in track, at least not since field day in grade school.

At a mile and a-half, a runner from Taylor came up on Cody's right shoulder. He sounded like he was hyperventilating, and he was holding his left side as he ran. He still left Cody behind him within a matter of seconds.

Cody felt his toes dragging as he came out of the first turn on lap seven. He looked ahead. It seemed that God had grabbed the track at either end and stretched it like it was made of taffy. The straight-away seemed to go on forever. He bowed his head.

I can't look ahead anymore, he moaned to himself. *It's too discouraging. Oh, super, who's this passing me now? Another guy from Taylor? He looks like he weighs about ninety-eight pounds. I feel like I weigh as much as Pork Chop.*

Cody wondered if it was a mirage when he saw Pork Chop waiting for him at the start of the final lap. "Code," he shouted as he started to jog along the infield, "I'm sorry, dawg. I fell asleep in the bus. Look, man, just one more lap to go. Piece o' cake. I'm gonna be right here beside you. I'll get you through it."

"Chop," Cody gasped, "please do me a—favor."

"Sure. Anything."

"Get—this blasted bear—off my back!"

"I wish I could, man. But you gotta fight him off yourself. Come on. Keep moving forward. You're almost there. Think how relieved you'll feel when you finish."

Cody heard the crowd start to scream as he entered the first turn of his last lap. He had to crank his head around as far as it would go to see Drew unleash a furious kick on the homestretch. Cabrera, who had stayed close the whole way, had no answer for it. He slowed to a jog as Drew dashed toward the finish line.

Cody glanced at his watch as he saw Drew cross the line and sink to his knees—11.29. He had the record, but barely.

Later, when Cody entered the homestretch, now in eighth place, he found Drew running beside him on the infield. "Come on Code," he rasped. "Almost home. First two miles behind you. The rest will be better. If you listen to me."

Cody smiled. He lengthened his stride and heard the timer call "Twelve-twenty-nine" as he loped across the line.

In the bus on the way home, Cody sat next to Drew, with Pork Chop behind them, hanging his thick forearms over the back of their seat.

"Yo, Flash," Pork Chop said, "is Cabrera really that close to you? I mean, I guess with that big mouth of his, he can suck a lot of oxygen."

"He's a good runner," Drew replied. "He's in good shape for this early in the year. But next time he won't be so close."

Pork Chop pounded the back of the seat with his palm. "Ha! I love your confidence, dawg. But are you sure?"

Drew nodded once. "Yeah. Today was just an experiment. I had to see what he was bringin'. I was going to put him away with two laps to go, but he said something to me. He said, 'I can outkick you anytime I want. You're mine!'"

Cody shook his head. "Man, I can't believe he said that—wait a minute—what am I saying? Of course I can believe it. It's Cabrera."

"So," Pork Chop said, "you let him hang with you, just so you could outkick him and show him up? That's beautiful! I think I'm gonna cry, that's so beautiful!"

"Thanks. But I have to correct you on one thing. I didn't do it to show him up. I did it to answer his challenge on his terms. To teach him a lesson. There's a difference. And speaking of lessons, Cody, you gonna give me eighty-nines next time?"

Cody smiled sheepishly. "Oh yeah, you can count on it. I was dying out there. The bear really got me."

"That's what happens when you go out too hot. If you'll run smarter, you'll outrun the bear."

"I don't know. I figure if I run long distance, he's gonna get me at some point."

"Not necessarily. Because when he closes in on you, you might just get your second wind."

Cody glanced out the window and watched the reflector poles whip by. "Second wind, huh? I thought that was kind of a myth."

Drew gave Cody a smile. "Some people think the bear is a myth, too."

Cody managed to avoid the bear for the next two meets. He worked hard to hit even splits and turned in a twelve-minute-flat 3200 at the Mill Creek dual, followed by an 11.56 at the Holy Family triangular.

Drew, meanwhile, established a personal best at Mill Creek, with an 11.22. And that was only about an hour after he turned in a 5.10 mile.

Grant held its annual quadrangular meet at the season's midway point, hosting Taylor, Mill Creek, and Central. Cody cringed when he saw his dad, in suit and tie on an eighty-degree day, patrolling the infield looking for him.

At least he doesn't have his woman with him, Cody thought. He had seen enough of Beth lately. She ate dinner at the Martin household two or three times a week. And Cody and his father had dined twice in Beth's closet-sized apartment. After their first meal at Chez Beth, she took the two of them into her bedroom. Her bed was covered with dozens of stuffed bears. She had named them all, and when she started describing when and how she had obtained each one, Cody felt like diving out a window.

Just as Cody finished congratulating Robyn on a personal best in the 200 meters, 29.2 seconds, good enough for third place, his dad spotted him.

"Cody! Hey, buddy-o, did I miss your race?"

"No, Dad, it's almost the last event of the meet. It won't be for another half hour, at least. You have time to go home and change."

"Why would I do that? This is a microfiber suit. It breathes."

Cody stared at his dad. *Am I really a blood relative to this guy?* he wondered. *I hope whatever he has skips a generation.*

Robyn touched the cuff of his father's suit. "That is a nice fabric, sir. It feels like it would be comfortable, for a suit, that is."

"Why, thank you, Robyn."

"You're welcome. Well, I better go find my home-girls and get some baton exchanges for our relay. Good luck in the 3200, Code."

Cody watched Robyn jog away. He wondered if he could run a twenty-nine-second 200 meters.

His dad's hand on his head interrupted his thoughts. "So, Son, you going to outrun 'em all today? Win one for the old man?"

Cody closed his eyes for a moment. He felt a headache coming on. "Gosh, Dad, put some pressure on me, why don't ya?"

"I'm only kidding, Cody. Just do your best and I'll be proud of you. You don't have to win."

"Well, that's good, because I'm not going to win. Drew won the mile—by almost a mile—a little bit ago, and he's going to do the same in the two-mile."

"Drew Phelps. Yes, he's a fine runner. You know, one of the guys over in sports at the paper said he's one of the fastest eighth graders in the state."

"Really, sir?" Drew said.

Cody blinked. He wasn't sure where Drew had come from. *I guess he's fast even when he's not racing,* Cody thought.

"Oh yes, Drew. There's a boy from Denver who is under five minutes, but you're very close to that, aren't you?"

"So close it hurts, sir. Maybe next week."

"Well, I'm looking forward to seeing you run today. And Cody, too, of course."

Drew pawed at the infield grass with his right spike. Then he frowned.

"What's up, D?" Cody asked. "You get some gum on your shoe?"

"No. It's just that my foot has been bothering me after the mile. Maybe I better go talk to Coach."

"I hope your friend is okay," Cody's dad said as Drew jogged away, slightly favoring his left foot.

Cody rubbed his hands together nervously. "Me, too."

When Cody heard the first call for the 3200, he surveyed the infield and the track, looking for Drew. He saw Goddard and Getman stretching in the high jump area and veered their way.

"Hey, guys, you seen Phelps? The two is coming up."

"No foolin', Martin," Goddard said. "I have to run it. I already did the mile. What's Coach trying to do, kill me?"

Cody cocked his head. "Why is he putting you in the two? We already have three guys in it—Bart, if he'll quit whining long enough to run, Phelps, and me."

"Scratch Phelps from that list," Getman said. "He says his foot is bothering him. I heard him tell Coach he thinks he should stay off it. And you know Coach isn't going to argue with his superstar."

"He seemed fine in the mile," Cody said, plopping to the ground and beginning to stretch. "Ran a 5.06 and looked really strong. Blew the field away. That really stinks if he can't compete. There go some easy first-place points. I wanted to win this meet, and I think Creek is almost dead even with us."

The second call for the race came while Cody ran pick-ups on the infield. Still no sign of Drew. Finally, as Coach Clayton switched on his bullhorn and droned, "Last call for the men's two-mile," Cody saw Drew walking slowly toward him. He curled his forefinger, signaling for Cody to approach.

"Your wheel really that bad, Flash?"

"Yeah, Code, I'm afraid so. But forget about that. Listen to me. This field is wide open."

"Yeah—now it is."

"Look, Code, we need the points, and I don't have to tell you we can't count on Goddard or Evans to finish in the money. But you—you could win this thing."

"Okay, forget your foot—something's wrong with your brain. Me? Win?"

"Yes, you. Believe it. Look, an 11.45 will win this."

"That's swell, Drew, but that's about fifteen seconds under my personal record."

"Yeah, but this is our home track. This is where we do our intervals. Just stay loose, Code. Relax. Run smooth and strong. Keep your splits even. And if you get in trouble, just hang in there and wait for that second wind."

"You keep talking about that. I haven't felt it all season."

"The season's not over yet. Now, go get 'em."

Cody trotted to the start line. "Nice of you to join us, Mr. Martin," Coach Clayton said. "Is it okay with you if we start the race now?"

Cody felt ten pairs of competitors' eyes on him. He knifed his way into the middle of the pack and waited for the gun.

As he finished the first lap, he kept his head down. He didn't want to meet the eyes of Pork Chop, his dad, or Robyn.

After three laps he was in fourth place. At the mile mark he slid ahead of a Mill Creek runner to take third. "5.45," Coach Clayton yelled as he passed by.

Third place, not bad, Cody told himself as he risked a glance behind him. He had separated from a chase pack, which was now about twelve yards behind him. Five yards ahead of him was Mack, who trailed the first-place runner from Taylor, by about ten yards. Third place would score points, and with no Creek runners ahead of him, give Grant a chance to win.

On lap six a little guy from Creek sped by Cody. Then, as his heart dropped in his chest, he saw him go by Mack and the runner from Taylor.

With a lap and a half to go, Cody looked to his left and saw Drew pacing him on the infield. "Code," he said urgently, "you can't be complacent here. Don't settle for placing when you can win. You gotta reel in that Creek guy or we could lose the meet!"

Cody flashed Drew a shocked look. He wanted to tell him off for applying so much pressure, but he dared not waste the oxygen.

As Cody headed into the final turn before the gun lap, Drew was still right beside him. "Cody, this is our home track. When you hit the straightaway, listen to the crowd yelling—all those car and truck horns honking. Feed off their energy. And let the second wind carry you!"

Cody saw the Taylor runner struggling as he completed lap seven. He rose on his toes and passed him as Coach Clayton shouted, "One lap to go, Code! Go get 'em, baby!"

Robyn, Cody's dad, and Pork Chop stood in the middle of the first turn of lap eight. All three were screaming, but Pork Chop's voice was the only one he heard clearly. "They're hurtin', dawg. They're meat if you put the speed on! Make 'em suffer! That's what we Raiders do, we make 'em suffer!"

Cody leaned into the turn, hugging it. Mack and the Creek kid were side by side, about seven yards ahead.

As Cody hit the backstretch, Drew appeared again. They ran stride for stride, neither saying anything. Then, with the finish line 240 meters away, Drew leaned toward Cody and barked, "Bust it! Now!"

As the word *now* exploded in his ears, Cody sensed a tingling in his head. He felt he had been running full out, but he realized he had at least one more gear. He rose up on his toes and found himself running with longer, quicker strides. He locked his eyes on the back of Mack's red-and-white singlet. As the lead twosome entered the final turn, Mack tucked behind the Creek runner.

Smart move, Cody thought. *You don't want to add to your distance by running wide through the turn.*

Suddenly Cody found himself on Mack's heels. There was still half a turn to go. Cody knew he should wait for the homestretch to make his move, but he felt strong. He was getting faster with each step, and he didn't want to dam the building momentum.

He swung wide of Mack and nudged ahead of him. He saw the surprise in Mack's eyes.

Cody stayed wide as he hit the homestretch. *No sense moving inside and then back out again to pass Creek*, he reasoned.

The kid from Creek whipped his head around and saw Cody, four yards behind and closing fast. They were fifty yards from the finish. The Creek runner churned his arms and went into his kick.

The kid from Creek was candy.

Cody launched himself into a full out sprint. He thought of sprinting downcourt in basketball to thwart a fast break. Of dashing downfield on a fly pattern, leaving the free safety reaching after him in futility.

With twenty-five yards to go, Cody pulled even with the lead runner. He saw the panic in the guy's eyes. He saw Drew and Gage holding a length of string across the two inside lanes. He leaned forward as he crossed the line, catching the string with his chest. He heard Drew screeching, his voice almost gone, "11.38! 11.38!"

The honking, cheering, and clapping rang in his ears. He saw Chop, Robyn, and his dad running toward him on the track ahead.

Second wind, huh? Cody thought as his dad swept him up in his arms. *Cool.*

With one arm around Pork Chop's shoulder and the other around Drew's, Cody let himself be walked across the infield.

"Stay on your feet," Drew instructed. "You don't even want to know what it's like to cramp up after running an 11.38 two-mile!"

"Are you sure that's right?" Cody asked, shaking his head.

"Got it straight from Coach."

"You better watch your back, Phelps," Pork Chop said. "My man here is gettin' his speed on!"

"I know. He's tough."

"Get real, Drew. You know you're still the man. And I wouldn't be where I am today without you. I sure couldn't have won today without you. Thanks for the encouragement."

"No problem."

Cody stopped walking and thought for a moment. "Hey, Drew, the way you ran along the backstretch, cheering me on?"

"Yeah."

"You were moving pretty good for a guy with a bad foot."

Drew winked and slid from under Cody's arm. He started running backward from where Cody and Pork Chop stood, staring dumbfounded.

"Yeah, it kinda started feeling better," Drew said, smiling. "Must be some kind of miracle!"

Pork Chop looked at Cody. "You don't think—"

Cody ran a hand through his cinnamon-colored hair. "I can't believe it."

Pork Chop smiled. "Look, Drew's over there shaking hands with your pops. Congratulating him on your victory, I bet. You church boys, you're something else."

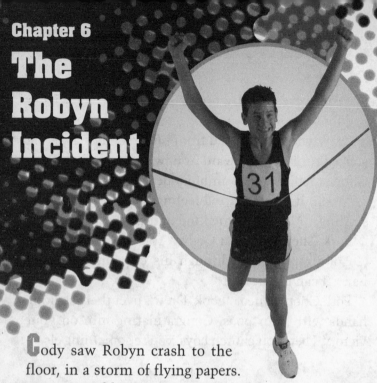

Chapter 6
The Robyn Incident

Cody saw Robyn crash to the floor, in a storm of flying papers.

He expected her to pop up, as she always did in basketball, and get in the face of Andrew Neale, who had tripped her.

But she stayed down. She wasn't moving.

Cody found himself sprinting toward her. He didn't remember breaking into a run. He only knew that Robyn was about thirty feet away now. Neale and his homeboy Rick Schutte stood nearby, laughing, but nervously.

Cody knew he should pray—quickly—for wisdom. This was one of those moments of truth Coach Clayton always talked about. But he didn't pray.

I don't want to hear an answer I can't obey, he admitted.

Schutte saw him bearing down first. He stepped back against a locker. Neale looked up as Cody closed in on him.

Cody remembered the Holy Family football game— the fourth-and-goal play at the one-yard line. The Saints had tried to send Mack over the top. Cody had studied the backfield and watched the play unfold. He left his feet only a second after Mack did. They crashed in midair at the half-yard line. Cody braced himself for impact. His left shoulder hit Mack in the midsection, and the ball popped free.

Marcus Berringer, who rounded the right end on a corner blitz, scooped up the fumble and was in the opposing end zone eleven seconds later. Berringer got the glory, but it was the hit that made the difference.

As Cody launched his body at Neale, he wondered what difference this hit would make. He raised his left elbow just before he made contact, hitting Neale square in the chest. That would have cost him a penalty in football, but this wasn't football. This was war. The impact sent Neale staggering backwards. He would have fallen, but he was caught by the Evans twins, who were approaching the scene as Cody hurled himself through the air.

Cody stuck out his right arm to brace his fall. He scrambled to his feet. Robyn was on her knees now, holding her left wrist with her right hand. It struck Cody that she resembled a referee signaling a holding penalty.

"Are you okay?" he asked.

"It's my wrist," she said weakly. "I'm afraid it's—"

That was all Cody needed to hear. He stalked toward Neale. "Come on. You and me," he said, trying to keep his voice in the lowest-possible register, "right now."

"Right now what?" he heard Mr. Prentiss say as he knelt by Robyn. "Mr. Martin, what's going on here? It's obvious that Robyn needs help. What are you doing that justifies not helping her?"

Cody searched for an explanation but found that his vocabulary had abandoned him.

"I can tell you what's up, sir," Neale said. "My feet accidentally got tangled up with Robyn's and she tripped. I was in a hurry, and I wasn't really looking where I was going. I'm sorry, Robyn. Really."

Robyn glared at him through eyes moist with tears. But she said nothing.

"And then," Neale continued, "Martin comes out of nowhere and blindsides me. It was a total cheap shot."

"You're a liar!" Cody spat. "I saw the whole thing. You couldn't leave it alone, could you?"

"That will be all, Mr. Martin," Mr. Prentiss snapped. "Head to my office right now. Everyone else, get to class."

When Mr. Prentiss turned his attention to Robyn again, Neale brushed by Cody. "You're dead," he whispered.

Cody watched his dad bang his folded-up *Wall Street Journal* on the arm of his recliner, as if he were trying to kill a stubborn spider. "Thanks for making my day, pal. There's nothing better than to be up to my neck in deadlines and stress, and get a call from the principal of your school, saying you started a fight in the hallway. What's up with you? Those pages about turning the other cheek fall out of your Bible? Or do you just ignore the stuff that's inconvenient for you?"

Cody stood before his dad, his hands jammed into his pockets. "I'm sorry, Dad. Please believe me. You gotta understand, though—this guy made life unbearable for that girl Greta. He's harassed Robyn all school year, and today he tripped her. He really hurt her. I saw it all happen, and I just snapped. I wasn't trying to start a fight. I was just trying to send him a message that he can't harass people the way he's been doing."

Cody's dad ran his hands through his hair.

"Cody, will you listen to yourself? You are a fourteen-year-old young man with a room full of citizenship awards. You call yourself a Christian. And yet you handle a problem by attacking a fellow student in the halls of your school?! What era do you think we're living in? This is civilization, Son. We don't solve our differences with clubs and spears anymore. If a fellow student does something wrong, you let the proper authorities handle it. I'm at a loss here. Has all that running depleted your brain of oxygen or what?"

Cody felt his head droop. "No sir. I know I did wrong. It's just that this punk Andrew Neale, he needed a lesson."

"And who appointed you his instructor? I'm really concerned here, Son. I hear you apologizing in one breath and then justifying your actions in the next. Listen to me—you—were—wrong."

"I know. I'm sorry. And I wasn't trying to justify what I did. I was just explaining why it happened. I'll handle things better next time. I promise."

"You better. This is humiliating. I never thought I'd have to deal with something like this with my son."

"I'm sorry."

"You should be. I hope you've learned from this. But, just to make sure you have, let's try a week with no TV."

"Okay, Dad."

Cody trudged up the stairs to his room. He dialed the Porters. He was relieved when he heard Pork Chop's voice.

"Dawg, I'm so disappointed in you."

"You too, huh?"

"You know it. You shouldn't have hit Neale with a flying elbow smash in the chest."

"I know, Chop. Believe me."

"Yeah—you shoulda aimed for his ugly pug nose. Or maybe his throat."

"You're crackin' me up, here, Chop."

"Dawg, I wished I woulda been there to see it. You're turning ghetto on me. There's hope for you yet."

"No, Chop. Look, you were right the first time. I was wrong to do what I did."

"Are you kidding me? Neale is a—"

"I don't want to hear it, Chop. I know what he is. But I was wrong. I think if Neale had been pushing Robyn around and I went to help her, I woulda been okay. Because I would have been protecting her, and the Bible says that love always protects. But I wasn't protecting her. In fact, I didn't even check to see how she was before I rocked Neale. It was like a reflex. I wasn't using reason. I just brought the war on him. I acted out of anger—out of revenge. Not because I was protecting someone."

"See, dude, this is why I'm not into religion. Too complicated."

"Doing the right thing is complicated sometimes. It's hard. But it's the right way."

"I feel what you're saying, dawg," Chop said. "I really do. But Neale needed a whupping. He just got what was comin' to him."

"But I was wrong to appoint myself teacher. And I don't think he learned anything. I think he's gonna come after me. I just stirred up a hornet's nest."

"Don't worry, Code. I got your back."

"I don't want to put that on you, Chop. It's not fair."

"Aww, you're trippin'. Fair? I'm your friend. Saving your scrawny white bod is one of my friend-like duties. Besides, squashing Andrew Neale? I get all tingly just thinking about it!"

"Look, Chop, I just hope the whole thing's over, at least for a while. We have districts coming up, and we need to focus on that."

"Maybe you're right. But I'm watching out for you, all the same."

"Thanks," Cody said. "You're a good friend."

"I know I am. That's why I won't tell everybody that a minute ago you uttered the words 'Robyn' and 'love' in the same breath."

As he hung up the phone, Cody frowned. "Did I?" he asked himself.

The week before the district meet, Drew finally cracked the five-minute-mile barrier. Coach Clayton had scheduled a low-key dual at Maranatha Christian School, but low-key wasn't part of Drew's athletic vocabulary. Maranatha had a fine half-miler named Shervin, who moved up to the mile to challenge Drew. Shervin pushed him hard for three laps, which the duo hit in seventy-five seconds each.

From the infield Cody saw Shervin's form start to break down on the backstretch of the gun lap. Drew pulled away, starting his kick with two hundred meters to go. He ran the final lap in seventy-three seconds, hitting the tape in 4.58.

Coach Clayton dashed to Drew, holding a stop-watch under his nose. He saw the coach give the watch to his star runner.

On the bus ride home, Drew sat transfixed, staring at the numbers. "Hey, Flash," Pork Chop called from the seat across from Drew, "when are you gonna quit gawking at that stopwatch?"

"As soon as the batteries wear out," was the quiet answer.

Central hosted the season-ending district meet,

which was fine with Drew. "This is the fastest track in the district," he said to Cody as they warmed up for the mile at midmorning.

"You got another sub-five in you?"

"Oh man, I hope so. I don't want to end the season with anything less."

The field for the mile was the biggest Cody had competed in. Nervously shifting his weight from foot to foot, he tried to count the runners assembled at the start line, but gave up, because the milling around made an accurate tally impossible.

He found a place in the middle of the pack and prayed he wouldn't be trampled at the start.

He needn't have worried. The pack quickly unraveled into an almost perfect single-file column, snaking its way around the track. Caught up in the excitement, a trio of Central runners sprinted to the lead. They held their position for one lap, before Drew, seeming irritated, dashed past them, followed by Shervin and Cabrera.

This duo shadowed Drew through lap two, which he hit in 2.29. Midway through the third lap, Drew surged ahead, as if someone had suddenly shoved him from behind. Neither Cabrera nor Shervin could cover his move.

Drew stretched his lead over the twosome to twenty yards by the time he crossed the finish line in

4.59. A district record but, to Drew's considerable irritation, not a personal record.

Shervin outkicked Cabrera for second. Cody finished seventh, in 5.32. He was disappointed not to place, but Drew reminded him that his time was only three seconds off what used to be the school record.

Perhaps using his failure to P.R. in the mile as fuel, Drew scorched the 800 meters. His 2.12 set a district record, bettering the old mark by three seconds. Shervin also finished under the old mark, clocking a 2.14.

Coach Clayton rubbed his hands together as he congratulated the two front-runners. "Fellas," he said, "I think we have the makings of a classic rivalry here. I'm gonna enjoy watching you two battle it out for four years in high school."

Because Drew had run the 800 and the 1600, he wasn't allowed to compete in the 3200. District rules prohibited any runner from racing in more than two events longer than 400 meters.

"It's a stupid rule," Drew observed as he helped Cody warm up for the two-mile. "I'm not even that tired. And I'd really love to run Cabrera into the ground one more time."

As Cody, Goddard, and Getman walked to the starting line together, Coach Clayton intercepted them.

"Okay, fellas, I'd love to see somebody get some points for us here. We're in second place, and I'd like to keep that position. It would mean another trophy for the case. But the important thing is to run a smart, steady race. Each of you. You know that some idiot is going to sprint at the beginning, just so he can tell his mommy, 'I was in first place, for a while.' Don't get sucked into that."

Cody and his running mates nodded in unison.

Moments later Cody could only shake his head when Getman charged to the front of the pack, battling for the lead with Cabrera and the little water bug from Creek, whose name, Cody had learned from Drew, was Winters.

As the early laps clicked by, Cody occasionally looked behind for Goddard and found him running steadily, about twenty-five yards back. Getman faded somewhere between laps one and two. Cody couldn't pick him out. Most of his attention, however, was ahead of him, on Winters and Cabrera, the only two runners he trailed as he hit the mile mark.

With two laps to go, he found himself thirty yards behind the leaders. He glanced quickly behind him. Mack was about ten yards back. He couldn't see Goddard anymore.

With one lap to go, Cody prayed for a second wind that would carry him closer to the front-runners. It didn't come. On the backstretch he heard Drew yell, "Hold your form! Keep working those arms! You're almost home!"

Cody did his best to obey. He saw Cabrera launch his kick as he came out of the final turn. Winters tried to keep up but he wasn't strong enough. Cody heard Mack's labored breathing behind him getting closer. He concentrated on quickening his pace.

On the homestretch Cody told himself, *Okay, unleash the kick now.*

But he found he had no kick left.

Fortunately, neither did Mack. It seemed to Cody they were both running in slow motion. He forced himself to lengthen his stride, straining to get some kind of advantage.

Cody crossed the line in 11.41, two seconds ahead of Mack. Third place. Good enough for a medal.

As the bus rumbled back to Grant, Pork Chop tried to free the Outstanding Athlete trophy from Drew's grip. "Come on, Flash, you know that should be mine. I have two gold medals, just like you. It's just that the weight men get no respect."

"I respect you," Drew affirmed. "But you're not gettin' my trophy."

Cody was sitting by himself near the back of the bus. Everyone wanted to sit by Drew. Cody watched athletes from the girls' and boys' teams take turns sliding next to him, admiring the gold medals and the trophy.

It's like he's the Pope or something, and everyone wants an audience with him, Cody laughed to himself.

Pork Chop was sitting by Jessica Adams, the sprinter who had entered the season a little soft but worked herself into shape. She placed second in the 200 meters and anchored Robyn's relay team to a silver-medal finish.

"Dude, I think Jessica likes me," Chop had told Cody as the athletes filed onto the bus.

"Chop, you think everybody loves you."

Pork Chop had spread his arms wide, as if he were on a stage, acknowledging an audience's thundering applause. "What's not to love?" he asked rhetorically.

Cody felt his eyes closing when Robyn slid into the empty seat next to him.

"Hey," she said. "Good race in the two. Third place isn't bad at all."

"It's not as good as second. How's your wrist? Did it do okay in the baton exchanges?"

"Yeah. It was fine. Where it bothered me most was in the start of the sprints. I couldn't put weight on it, so I had to go from a standing start. That kinda messed me up."

"But you still placed in the 100 and the 200. The relay, too."

"Yeah. But Jessica's still the rock star of the sprints."

"Kinda like Drew is at distance. Hey, I'm sorry again about Neale. I wish I could have been there sooner. To at least, uh, catch you or something."

Robyn smiled. "Well, you had my back, as best you could. What did that little flying elbow smash end up costing you, anyway?"

Cody whistled through his teeth. "Four in-school detentions. Ninety minutes each. Mr. Prentiss said it woulda been much worse if it hadn't been my first offense—only offense—in almost three years."

"Still, that's pretty harsh."

"I just wish Neale would let it go. I mean, he already chased Greta out of school. He won, you know? Why is he still pushing it?"

"I don't know, Cody. I mean, I read him the riot act in front of a crowd. You called him out in the hallway, and then you decked him. He's a hothead and a loud-mouth. I don't know if we've seen the last of him. Maybe it's time to call in the big guns."

"You mean Pork Chop."

"Well, he does have arms like Vin Diesel," Robyn said, "and he doesn't mind scrappin'. And since reason really didn't work—maybe Pork Chop can be like one of the judges in the Old Testament."

"Yeah, but Robyn, I don't want to always have to fall back on him. He's been watchin' my back since before I had all my permanent teeth. I have to learn to solve at least some of my own quarrels without him. I mean, what's he going to do? Grow up and get a job as my bodyguard?"

"What makes you think you're going to need a bodyguard?"

"Don't all NBA players have bodyguards?" Cody asked.

"Oh, brother, it's gettin' deep back here. I'm out. I'm going back to the front of the bus. Back to Reality Land."

Robyn stood and began making her way forward, using the seats on either side for balance. Cody watched her but quickly turned his head when she turned around.

"Seriously, though, dawg,'" she said, smiling. "Good running today. And thanks for coming to my rescue—again."

Cody saluted and checked the pocket of his sweats to make sure his medal was still there.

"Okay, I think you're officially brain-dead now," Cody told Drew as they jogged from the school. "Didn't we get enough running in today?"

"Code, it's just a couple-mile warm-down. After more than an hour cramped up in the bus, we need it.

Trust me. You'll be less sore tomorrow."

Cody listened to the sound of his sweatpants whooshing together as he ran. "Okay, " he conceded. "But just a couple miles."

Cody and Drew were headed east on Main Street, crossing the parking lot of Chuck's Used Cars, when the foursome attacked. Cody recognized the battered Nova immediately, as Weitz gunned the engine, cut in front of them, and then squealed to a stop. Neale and Schutte spilled out of the backseat. Weitz and a skeleton-like high school senior Cody knew, but not by name, exited from the front doors.

"This way!" Drew commanded, grabbing Cody by the front of his track singlet and flinging him away from their attackers.

Schutte, Neale, and the living corpse gave chase immediately. Cody, whipping his head over his shoulder, saw Weitz start to get back in his car, then change his mind and start running.

"Weitz, you oversize freak!" Cody heard Drew yell. "Come on—just try to catch me!"

Cody shot Drew an "Are you crazy?" glare as they sprinted out of the parking lot and toward the dilapidated apartment buildings and mobile homes that lurked behind Main Street on the east side of Grant.

"We gotta split up," Drew snapped, his voice way too strong for someone running at full speed. "I'm

going to keep heading south. There's a bunch of con-
struction going on. I'll be able to lose 'em. You—"

"I'm gonna head east," Cody gasped.

"Yeah?"

"Yeah."

"Okay," Drew said, nodding, "Now!"

Cody watched Drew skid to a stop for a moment,
letting the attacking quartet draw close. "Come on,
Weitz," he half-growled. "If you're man enough." Then
he was off again, regaining top speed in only a few
strides.

Meanwhile Cody peeled off and cut left, just as if
he were running a down-and-out pattern. He risked a
look back. Neale and Skeleton Boy were on him. He
felt adrenaline coursing through his body as he led his
chasers across Highway 7, into a land of trees and
deep weeds. A land he remembered well.

As he followed Clear Creek, watching the ground
in front of him for rocks or fallen branches, he heard
a loud gasp. He turned and saw Skeleton Boy, bent
over, hands on his knees, gulping for air. He was done.

Neale still gave chase, however. And Cody was
beginning to feel his leg muscles tightening. His heart
jackhammered in his chest, and there didn't seem to
be enough oxygen in the early evening air to supply
his needs.

God, he prayed, *I know you didn't bring me a second wind during the race today. So I'm wondering if maybe now would be a good time.*

Cody looked behind him. Neale was closing in, breaking into a do-or-die sprint.

"Come on, Neale," he managed to wheeze. "If you can catch me, I'm probably dead. Districts—took everything out of me."

With that, Cody threw himself down a hill, toward the clearing where the bus that Greta and her family lived in had once rested. He tumbled to the bottom of the hill and then scrambled to his feet. As he watched Neale bear down on him, he felt the power of the second wind fill his body.

He saw Neale's chest heaving as he staggered toward him.

Cody flung himself at Neale. He could feel the air go out of his opponent as he crash-landed on his chest.

Seconds later he found himself sitting on Neale's stomach, glaring down at him. In his left hand, he held a balled-up handful of Neale's black T-shirt. His right fist was cocked by his ear. He watched Neale blink and focus his eyes before he spoke.

"You're spent, dude. You know it and I know it. But I—I feel strong. Like I could battle all day."

Neale tried to say something, but all that escaped his lips was, "Whuh—"

"Shut up. Don't even try to talk. Just listen. You know where we are? Greta used to live here, until *you* chased her away. She was innocent, and you terrorized her. Now you're gonna pay."

Cody saw genuine fear rise in Neale's eyes. He wanted to drive his fist down across that broad, flat nose, scattering flecks of blood everywhere. But, somehow, an image of David, King Saul, and an incident in a cave flashed into his brain.

He relaxed his grip on Neale's shirt. But he kept his fist locked and loaded, just in case. "You believe in God, Neale?"

Neale blinked his eyes and then shook his head no.

"Well, you should. Because he just saved you from the beating of your life. He's the only thing keeping me from turning your face to hamburger. And there's nobody here to help you. And what I could do to you doesn't even compare to what Pork Chop wants to do. But I'm not gonna let him."

Warily, Cody rose from Neale's stomach. "This ends, here, okay? It's over. You've done enough damage. I've tried to turn the other cheek. But I'm fresh outta cheeks. You even give Robyn a dirty look, and I promise I'll put a big hurt on you. Then I'll call Pork Chop. And you know what he can do."

He extended a hand toward Neale. Neale didn't take it. Instead he rolled to his side and pushed himself to his feet.

Cody stared him down. "Are we clear on this? It's over, right?"

Neale met Cody's eyes for a moment and then looked at the ground. "Yeah, it's over. Unless you go shooting your mouth about what happened here. I gotta maintain my pride, ya know."

"I'm not saying a word about this to the kids at school."

"I can live with that. But what about Weitz? He's the one who kinda recruited me and Schutte to help find you."

Cody exhaled thoughtfully. "I don't know about him. I might have to talk to my dad—or Doug Porter—about that."

"Doug Porter? Okay, then, I'm done with Weitz. You tell Porter I have nothing to do with Weitz, okay?"

Cody paused for a moment.

Neale's eyes widened. "Okay?!"

"Okay," Cody said quietly.

Chapter 7

Going for a Ride

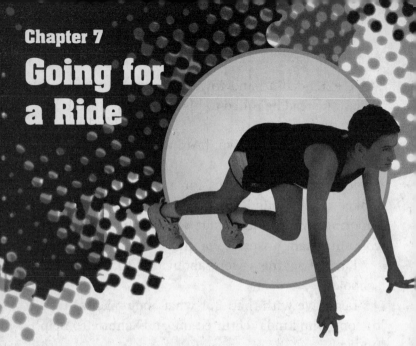

Cody ran west along Main Street, in the dying light of the day. His head rotated from side to side, watching for Weitz's Nova—or a sign of Drew.

He leaped a foot in the air when he heard the two quick beeps of a horn behind him. He spun around to face the car, then took a deep breath when he saw Terry Alston and his mother in the front seat of a sea-blue Corolla.

Alston poked his head out the driver's-side window. "Hey, Martin, what's the deal? You some kind of masochist?"

"I'm just warming down. Hey, good race, by the way. Mean hundred meters."

"Yeah, I'm just bummed I let Nakamura beat me. Guy's a mutant."

Cody nodded. "Still, twelve flat, that's smokin'."

Alston chuckled. "Yeah, I guess so. Hey, you want a ride? I'm legal and all. Learner's permit. Right, Mom?"

Cody thought for a moment. "Sure, I guess so."

"Well, jump in, then. I'm burnin' gas here."

Cody crawled into the backseat. He saw Alston watching him in the rearview mirror as he waited for the traffic to clear.

"Mom," he said, "this is Cody Martin."

Mrs. Alston twisted around in her seat and extended a slender hand. "Hello, Cody. Terry talks a lot about you."

Cody almost snorted and said, "No way!" but he was too stunned, or too tired, for such a comeback.

"Terry says you can really play basketball. Says he thinks you guys can win state by the time you're through with high school."

"Cody runs track with me, too, Mom. He placed at districts today, in the two-mile!"

Mrs. Alston smiled. "Really? That's great. Your parents must be proud."

Terry Alston leaned across the seat. "Mom," he whispered through gritted teeth.

"Oh my goodness, that's right. Oh, Cody, I'm so sorry. Please forgive me. That was a really insensitive thing to say."

Cody contorted his face into the "brave smile" he had almost perfected. "That's okay, ma'am. Actually, I think you're right. They are proud. It's just that my dad is proud from earth, and my mom is proud from heaven."

He saw Mrs. Alston dip her hand into her purse and fish out a pale-pink tissue. She dabbed at her eyes. "Oh, my. That is a beautiful thought."

Cody sat back in the seat. *It is beautiful,* he thought.

"Hey, Code," he heard Alston saying. "I want you to know I'm sorry about Neale tripping Robyn a while back. I should have said something to him then, but I'm going to have a talk with him. What he did—that was weak."

"Andrew Neale tripped a girl?" Mrs. Alston asked. "Just wait till he comes over to our house. He's tripped his last person, I can assure you of that. Terry, that kid is nothing but trouble. I don't know why you hang out with him."

"Sometimes I don't know, either, Mom," Alston muttered.

When the car stopped at a traffic light, Mrs. Alston turned to Cody again. "Listen to me, if there is anything we can do for you or your dad, please let us know. We want to help, truly."

Cody eyed the road ahead as the light turned green. "Actually, there is something you can do. See that guy running up there, turning off Main to head for the school? He's a friend of mine. Maybe you could give him a ride, too?"

"Yeah—that's Drew Phelps, Mom, the distance ace. Hey, Code, I bet it's helped you a lot, having a teammate like that."

Cody smiled. "Yeah, it has. I owe him a lot. By giving him a ride, you can help me start paying him back."

He opened the door as the car crawled to a stop. "Phelps," he said, "your ride's here, man."

Drew slid into the seat, introduced himself to Mrs. Alston, and nodded at Terry. He sat back and fastened his seatbelt.

Cody studied his friend. "They catch up with you?"

Drew winked at him and smiled. "Are you *kidding* me?"

"Amen," Cody whispered.

He lay on his bed, staring up at the light above him. He closed his eyes and breathed deeply. Dinner was good. Beth was getting better at the whole spaghetti thing. And she wasn't as into over-describing the food as she used to be.

His latest prayer was one of thanks—acknowledging God for delivering him and Drew from Weitz and his posse. Weitz was still going to be a problem, but Cody had loved the look on his dad's face when he related the whole saga.

In fact, Dad had looked downright Clint Eastwood-like when he leveled his eyes at Cody and said, "Son, let me handle this. I'll take care of it. That's a promise."

Cody slid his hand into his sweatpants' pocket and retrieved his bronze medal. He held it up to the light, turning it first to the left and then to the right. He smiled. If you held it right, the bronze looked just like gold.

SPIRIT
OF THE
GAME

15

Will Cody
survive
the cut?

STEALING HOME

BY TODD HAFER

Zonderkidz

Chapter 1

Real Angels Throw Fastballs

Cody shielded his eyes with his right hand, his cinnamon-colored hair peeking out from under his ball cap, as he tracked the tiny sphere arcing against the midday Colorado sky. When it reached its zenith, he lost it for a moment. But then, as it dropped back toward earth, his eyes found it again. He slid to his right and waited. He risked a glance at Blake, who was staring at him in bewilderment.

He's wondering why I'm not moving under the ball, mitt up to catch it, Cody thought, laughing to himself. The ball was picking up speed now, looking as if it would thud on the grass to Cody's left. He stood, arms dangling at his sides, as the ball hurtled past his head.

Then, just as the ball was level with his hip, Cody crouched and stabbed his outfielder's mitt to the left—and snagged it only a foot from the ground.

"Had you worried, didn't I?" he said, chuckling.

Blake shook his head. "Nah, Code, I just thought you lost the ball in the sun."

Cody flipped the ball from his glove to his right hand. Then, with a flick of his wrist, he whipped a hard grounder to his youth pastor Blake. Blake dropped to his knees and scooped the ball into a well-worn softball mitt, his "church-league special," as he called it. Then he stood, rocked back, and fired a fastball that zoomed toward Cody's face.

Cody yawned. The ball bulleted toward him, less than ten feet from his nose now. He waited as long as he could and then snapped his glove hand up to his face, as if to swat a horsefly. The ball hit his glove with a deep smack.

"Yeow!" he yelled, letting the mitt slide off his hand, which he shook and flexed, curling and uncurling his fingers. "You had some mustard on that one, B!"

Blake flexed his right bicep. "Yeah, pretty good hose for a guy who plays only church-league softball, huh?"

Cody nodded. "Not bad. But watch this!" He went into an elaborate stretch. His eyes bored into Blake.

He shook off two signals from an imaginary catcher, then planted his left foot and brought his arm forward like a bullwhip.

He tried to reign in a smile when he heard the pop of the ball in Blake's mitt less than two seconds later.

"You know," Blake said as he bounced a bumpy grounder toward Cody, "biblical legend has it that some angels did this with the stone used to seal Jesus' tomb—after the Resurrection."

Cody cocked his head. "You're kidding, right? Angels played baseball? The only baseball-playing angels I've heard of are the ones in Anaheim."

Blake nodded. "Well, some people believe different. I know it sounds far-fetched, but think about it. That huge stone weighed about two thousand pounds—as much as your dad's car. It would have taken a bunch of guys with levers to move it into a groove in the bedrock of the tomb.

"Then it was sealed with wax, and that signified that a burial was final. Whoever was inside the tomb wasn't going anywhere."

Cody squinted against the sun as he sidearmed the ball toward Blake. "B," he said, "do *you* believe that legend, or whatever it is?"

Blake grinned and pitched the ball back to Cody. "You know, I kinda do. I mean, think about it. Jesus came to life—after two days inside a dark tomb.

Maybe he pushed that huge stone out of the way himself, or maybe the angels did it. In either case, those angels had to be amped. And what better way to celebrate than toss around the very stone that was supposed to be massive enough to seal their Lord's eternal fate?"

"You have a point." Cody fired the ball again. "Do you think the angels could throw a banana curveball like that one?"

Blake caught the toss. He hesitated for a moment, then plucked the ball from his mitt, tossing it up and down in his right hand as if it were an egg that was too hot to handle. "I'm sure they could," he said, "but I have a feeling they didn't. Think about it. Your Lord and Master has just defeated death itself, and you're standing there at ground zero, toying with the boulder that was supposed to imprison him forever. Nah, I think in that case, you gotta throw the high, hard cheese. Like this!"

ISBN 0-310-70671-8

Available now at your local bookstore!

Zonder**kidz**

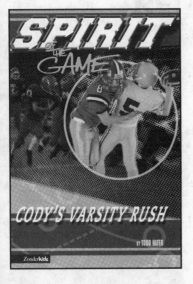

We want to hear from you. Please send your comments about this book to us in care of zreview@zondervan.com. Thank you.

Zonder**kidz**®

Grand Rapids, MI 49530
www.zonderkidz.com